A Dad's Redemption

A Dad's Redemption

By Renetta C Gunn-Stevens

Copyright© 2014 by Renetta C Gunn-Stevens

Published by Sophisticated Press

PRINTED IN THE UNITED STATES OF AMERICA

Book Design by Janice Recede

ISBN 978-0-9988669-1-8

Published by Sophisticated Press

Po Box 831 Elmhurst IL, 60126

For more information see

Website: Sophisticatedpress.com

Email:sophisticatedpress@gmail.com

SOPHISTICATED
PRESS

Acknowledgments

It feels so good to finally see the manifestation of your dreams. This book has been in the incubator of mental creativity for a long time. Without the support and inspiration of a few mentionable individuals this book would still be a thought. So without further or do here are my acknowledgements. To my husband Kelvin Stevens, thank you for allowing me to disturb your sleep at night with the light from my laptop and clicking from my typing. You have supported me in every assignment and dream that God has given and for that I say thank you. You are my customized soulmate from Heaven. To my children Kierra, Kelvin Jr, & Kameryn, thank you for understanding when mommy had to lock herself in a room and "work". To my parents Dorise & Raymond Gunn, thank you for providing me a safe and loving childhood that allowed me to dream, imagine, and plan my future. Thank you mom for introducing me to Jesus Christ. Thank you for being my inspiration and my rock. If I can become half the woman that you are I will be content. To my sister Schlise Browley, thank you for always cheering me on and being my role model. To Moe, thank you for always playing with Kam and being a wonderful husband to my sister. To my youngest brother Dupree, you are my best friend and always keep me learning. I appreciate your genius. To my oldest brother Lamont, thank you for your sincere heart and your deep conversations. To Carl, thank you for being one of the coolest brothers a sister could ask for. To Maurice, Cheryl, Destini, Tequela & Bo Bo love y'all. To Isaac, Nicole, Pat, & De-De (RIP) thank you for being great cousins to me. To my best friends Nicole B, Latasha G, and Shawana, thank you all for loving me and supporting me in all of my entrepreneur endeavors. To LaQuanda Smith. thank you for also assisting me with editing and being my personal motivator when doubt crept in. To Brianna and Curtis thank you for being beautiful people that I get to be an Aunt to. To Matthew N. & Denise N. your passion for communication inspired me to write more and become vulnerable while presenting my creativity. To Pam DeFiglio, thank you for reading the manuscript and assisting with editing. To the Stevens family thank you for all of your support and inspiration. Your feedback gave me fuel to complete the task. To Janice Recede thank you for sharing your genius with the book cover. To Gina & Russel, thank you for your support and loving kindness. To Olivia & Yvonnda thank you for being my sisters and sharing laughs and cries with me. To everyone that reads this book I encourage you to write a book. Don't write a book only for profit. Write to leave your legacy and your finger print in time. A wise man once said that "Dead men rule the world by the books they have written". Join their reign! Lastly, to CHICAGO, CHI-TOWN, & THE WINDY CITY thank you for having me as a citizen and being the back dropped to my memories, future, and destiny.

Renetta C Gunn-Stevens

Contents

Chicago I

The Land of The Brave and Beautiful

Summertime in Chicago Illinois is a culture concoction of holidays and homicides. Pop-up barbecue grills, Cops, and teddy bears with empty alcohol bottles on corners are the accessories to neighborhoods. Parks become late night breeding grounds for one-night stands and showcases of the latest edition of tricked out antique vehicles. Dodging potholes becomes a sport and not being attacked by the windshield wiper man at the stop light is a gift from God. At least that's how it is in my neighborhood. I live on the west side of Chicago in the Austin area. In the winter, mid-February, you pray for 80-degree weather to arrive while your toes unthaw from the ten inches of snow fallen in two hours and 30 mph winds. After the Lord answers your prayers with sunshine, muggy nights, butterflies, mosquitos, and plushy green grass that tickle your toes you immediately begin to reconsider the prayer due to the repetitive sounds of sirens, heighten gun violence, and the loss of love ones to heat strokes. This is the cycle of my life as a Chicagoan.

Chicago is known for celebrities like Oprah, Larenz Tate, and Bernie Mac. I believe we have the best pizza in the world. Garrets cheese and caramel popcorn is the best union after Michael Jordan and the Chicago Bulls. I am a true Chicagoan, born and raised in the Cabrini Green complex apartments on the near north side. These apartments were referred to as "row houses" and had a bad image portrayed by media and other social outlets. As a child growing up in the projects, I had no clue I was living in a "war zone" or a "blood pool" as some would call it. I do remember coming home from church with mama after New Year Eve's watch night when I was six years old and the police had our community blocked off so other Chicagoans could not drive through. Everyone was afraid of Cabrini Green projects except the residents. It was a small community where everyone knew you by your name. They had permission to discipline you if you were acting a fool and your parents would not mind or call the police. In fact growing up as a child I preferred the neighbors to chastise me versus my parents. Mama took all the love out of whippings. As a child I would look her dead in the eyes during whippings to remind her that it was her precious baby she was beating. The truth is they weren't really beatings. My heart and pride hurt more than my hide. My Pa would just look at me and the fear of his striking created whelps on my bottom and my legs.

My name is Kendra Latrice Springfield and on Friday June 4, 2010 my best friend Trina and I made our mothers proud by graduating from high school without babies. It wasn't hard. Most of the guys at William Jameson High were jerks, game freaks, or not interested in girls who had goals. Besides, Shelia Westbrook had a baby in the junior year and James Hellum went ghost on her. Excuse my Chicago lingo, "ghost" means he disappeared. All that kissing at the basketball games and holding hands in the hallways ended with

Sheila having a wide nose, big belly, and a transfer to an alternative school. Meanwhile, James was free to hunt for another victim.

Soon it will be daisy dukes season and time to show some legs. My mom always asks, "Who is Daisy and where is Dukes?" I have to remind her that daisy dukes are a term we call shorts that stop right after your buttocks. Today I erased my cell phone alarm for 6:15 a.m. and it was monumental.

They say opposites attract so I guess that is why Trina, my best friend and I get along so well. Some people describe me as sweet and Trina as spicy. Trina is a Diva to her heart. She wears only MAC lip gloss, ALDO shoes, Coach perfume, shimmery clothes, and Gucci sun glasses. Now some may wonder where she gets the money to wear such expensive items. Trina's mom gives her an allowance of $200 every two weeks. Her mom, Ms. Sara, over compensates her with money since her career as a Web Developer keeps her traveling and never at home. She feels guilty that Trina's older sister Sasha has moved to another state due to an open market at her job as a Real Estate Broker. Ms. Sara is the only one on the block with a Mercedes Benz. She parks it in their garage in the back of the house. It is magenta red and the license plate reads BOSSCHIC. When she comes home from work her top is always down on the convertible and her long straight black hair is perfect as if the wind is afraid to blow on it. She always wears high heels and owns one pair of gym shoes which is for the treadmill only.

Trina's philosophy is to attract a million bucks you have to look like a million bucks. In her case almost spend a million bucks too. I want to attract a million bucks, but I shop at the secondhand store. I call it goodwill couture. At a young age my grandmother Lillie revealed to me that one woman's trash is another woman's treasure. I tried to introduce Trina to this theory of shopping at the second-hand store but she sneezes and her eyes gets red and puffy when we walk the aisles. She proclaims she is allergic to cheap. She made me promise not to take her there again.

This summer is going to be bitter sweet because we have been accepted to different colleges. I've been awarded a choir scholarship to Eastern University. After attending school together since the sixth grade we are splitting up. Trina is going to study fashion at The Art Institute of California. We've made a pact to spend at least four days out the week together this summer which will be easy because she is my BFF and we live on the same street, West Park Ave.

Every day on our block is a drama scene. It's Friday and I am looking forward to doing my routine trip to Trina's porch at 6:30 p.m. The sun is beginning to tuck in the clouds and the heat is a little more bearable. Trina is already out waiting for me sitting on the top of the stairs. Trina and I don't partake in a lot of activities. I don't know if it is by preference or exposure. It seems like tourist know exactly where all the happening spots or events are and we "the locals" are oblivious to them. It may sound boring but some of our best laughs and cries have been on her porch. It's our safe haven. We both have our driver licenses, but our moms have only one car and they are both occupied during the day. Every Saturday we go shopping at the malls and catch a matinée movie. Sometimes Ms. Sara will give us the keys to drive the Benz but it always seems to attract older men.

While walking towards her house I began to notice the unusual silence of the block. No one is getting a boot on their car for unpaid parking tickets or moving away from the neighborhood due to violence or evictions. There is no loud music rattling from the trunks of Chevy's, Monte Carlos, or Regal Buicks as they drive by. Nino, the chief of the neighborhood gang, and his crew are not wearing their customary white t-shirts on the corner in front of the hardware store. Mr. Wilson the owner has told them several times to vacate the premises, but they just ignore his plea and vanish when the police arrive. Mrs. Cecil, the nosy neighbor, isn't sitting on her porch eating a bowl of fresh cantaloupe or looking out her window. The weirdest of all, Thirsty Ted, the neighborhood alcoholic, has not walked by and asked to borrow his economically friendly fifty cents. You knew if those two quarters left your hands you would never see them again.

Trina and I began to notice all these weird inconsistencies of the day. At the same time while opening her gate we said in unison "Where is everyone at?"

"Jinx," I said lightly pushing Trina shoulder.

Trina looked at me with disgrace and said, "Kendra really… really jinx. "Ima need you to catch up to 2010."

"Did anyone get shot today?"

"I don't know" Trina answered as she flicked her thumb and looked through her daily texts to see if she overlooked a neighborhood e-blast warning us which streets to stay clear of due to gun violence.

"Ken, is there a basketball game on?"

"No, basketball season ended yesterday. Trina, the Lakers beat the Celtics 83 to 79. Ima need you to catch up on your sports Diva. Especially if you plan on marrying Derrick Rose one day."

"Don't try to get me back because you used jinx, a term from 1987."

"Whatever Trina," I said while rolling my eyes.

Trina and I was the only two out on the block sitting on porches.

"I can't believe it is Friday and no one is out."

"I know right. Kendra you don't understand. I have been saving this outfit all week just for today and now I can't wear it again until at least another two weeks. Somebody has to see me today and when I say somebody you know I mean "everybody", we said in unison. Trina began admiring herself in her silver pocket mirror and looking in the reflection of her glass front door.

"I don't know why you think you can't do a repeat on the outfit, no one is out here so you can get away with it if you wear it again on Wednesday."

"Do you see me Ken? This is not a Wednesday outfit… OK" Trina reminded me by turning around to give me a chance to reflect on how fly she was. Trina give everyone a nickname. She was wearing the new summer collection of PINK. Her leggings were black with the mandatory glitter down the seams. Her shoes were from Nike. She knew she was an eye catcher today, so I decided to give Trina her daily dose of recognition.

"Yeah you right, that outfit is a show stopper, but you know me I would pull it. Guys get away with wearing the same outfit for three freaking days in a row. Remember Kyle? He wore his black and red jogging suit with the matching Air Jordan's a whole week. No one questioned his hygiene?"

"Kyle has a set of balls Ken."

"And?"

"So, Kyle can get away with that foolishness. Even if I could get a pass, I would not take it. Fashion is my passion."

There was no need for a rebuttal. Trina would never wear the same outfit twice in a week or month, so I begin to check my wardrobe as well. I wasn't doing so bad myself. My Levi short set is also an eye catcher. My shorts are one-inch shy of my mother demanding they be thrown away or worn as underwear. I have the daintiest white tank top on that makes the dark blue dye in the denim intensify. It is leg season. Playing four years of basketball as point guard has my legs strong, smooth, caramel, hairless, and sculptured. My shoes are from Madden Girl and they are fresh out the box. Quickly I do a boob check to make sure the girls are even to the eye if you know what I mean. But all this checking did not matter. On any good day Trina was the Diva and I am the Diva in training. This is my position. I have accepted it and play it well.

Our friendship works because we have a lot in common. We both like R. Kelly, fashion, reality T.V., and both of our dads are dead. My Pa is really dead due to a heart attack six years ago on the job at a construction site. Trina's dad is alive but he left her mom when she was two years old due to drug usage, so to her he is dead. I'm not saying it is right but that's her perception. Trina has something that I always wanted... a front porch. Trina's porch was the customary hub for gossip sessions as well as meeting grounds before any and every occasion. It was conveniently located in the middle of the block where you could see everyone in their daily activities. For the life of me I cannot figure out why my Pa purchased a building without a front porch, but I'm grateful and enjoy having my own room. I have something Trina always wanted …. a close relationship with my mom and a slow temper. Some see it as a sign of strength others a sign of weakness. I'm just practicing what I was taught by my mom to honor thy mother and father and to follow peace with all men. Trina always asks me, "Kendra why you let people talk to you like that? Why you don't go H.A.M on them."

H.A.M. is the abbreviation for hard as a motherf*#&@%. Trina picks up on my slow responses early and does what a real friend would do; she protects me and shelter me. On any good day she will step in front of me and finish an argument or take over a conversation. She'll say, "Let me handle this, you ain't mad enough." Trina is a firecracker in silk clothing. I don't mind Trina's protection because my oldest sister Krystal and I are not that close. She got married and moved away from home six years ago, right after Pa died. She left me to fend for myself with unanswered questions like, how to kiss a boy, how to insert a tampon, and when do you know you are ready for the big "S"…sex? Now, according to the Bible marriage is when you are ready for sex, but I do not live in Egypt or Jerusalem. I live in Chicago where the pressure and competition are always on and I feel like I am losing the race waiting on Jesus to send me a boyfriend as a potential husband. I'm sure I could call Krystal and ask her these things, but she would probably laugh at me first and make it uncomfortable to continue the conversation. I can hear her now in my head, "Who you trying to kiss" or "aww my little sister is not a virgin anymore." No thank you to that conversation.

Trina lost her virginity at age 16 so I get all of my information from her. She got all her information from her older sister Sasha. Sasha is twenty-three years old and engaged to a guy who is a professional landscaper. Her extra five years of life and wisdom has helped Trina and I maneuver through life. Trina told me that sex is overrated and the boy sweats and makes ugly faces and noises. "Your virginity is special so save it for someone special and who doesn't sweat" she constantly tells me. She says a little sweat is normal, but one guy had sweat dripping from his face and forehead and it got in Trina's hair. So, she said since then she always rides the driver seat in the car if you know what I mean. As I sit back down on the porch I begin to shake my leg uncontrollably. When I'm nervous, bored, sleepy, or excited this is therapeutic for me. Today I am bored and curious to where everyone is.

"Excuse me ladies I don't mean any harm but if you can see it in your heart to loan me fifty cents that's it?

"Thirsty Ted I mean Ted!" I blurted with excitement to see a familiar face after two hours of sitting on the porch.

Thirsty Ted is the nicest alcoholic you could ever meet. His clothes carry the smell of fabric softener and vodka. He is the only alcoholic I know who gets his pants heavy starched at the cleaners. His gray and white hair is always in a clean shave and cut because he is the custodian of the neighborhood barber shops and receive free haircuts for his work. We call him Thirsty Ted because he is always craving for alcohol or money to buy alcohol. He is a sweetheart and the neighborhood protect him when he is staggering down the street and ignores him when he is talking crazy and soliciting fights. His politeness displays his southern hospitality. He is originally from Chicago but landed a job in Memphis Tennessee and migrated back to Chicago after his divorce from his wife. He often shared how drinking helps him endure the pain of being separated from his only daughter Linda and losing a good job as an electrician.

"Where is everyone at Ted?" Trina asked.

"What is today's date?" Ted asked while looking at an imaginary calendar in the sky.

"June 18th." I blurted while taking the short cut and looking at my phone.

"Big Lou is having a surprise party tonight. Everyone is at his house in the basement waiting for him to get home from work. Kendra, I gave your mom the invitation last week while helping her bring in some groceries from the car, you didn't get it?"

"Now Ted, mama is getting old and can't remember like she used to. That invitation probably got tore apart and used to light the stove." I replied shaking my head and laughing at the same time.

Trina interrupted and asked for Big Lou address. Ted scratch his head and begin to murmur, "25...2502 N. Main St. you can't miss it. He has the only red house on the block. If you all are going by you better get there by a quarter to eight because Big Lou gets home by 8:30-9 p.m."

We stood up and Trina began to lock her door and Thirsty Ted said, "Will one of you beautiful young ladies be able to help me with that fifty cents?"

"Here's a dollar Ted because you just made our day." As all three of us began to walk out the gate Trina locked it and we began to walk toward Big Lou's house. Ted darted toward the liquor store. He knew about all the neighborhood events but never attended them.

Chicago II

The Land of Possibilities

"**K**endra, I knew something was strange about today. I was going to ask you to pinch me so I could wake up." Trina said, while we sprinted to Big Lou's house to beat his arrival.

"This must be the house Ken."

It was a big red brick house with custom white painted tire flower pots.

"Which bell do we ring Ken?"

"I guess the bottom one. Thirsty Ted said everyone was in the basement, remember?"

I shrugged while pressing the last button that had a dim yellow glow to it. Suddenly two big brown eyes appeared from behind the eggnog colored lace curtains on the oval glass and wooden door. It was Big Lou's mom Estelle Washington. She is 5'3 in stature but a giant at heart. She is a proud member of Mt. Calvary Baptist Pilgrim Church and has bragged in the past at the laundromat on not missing a Sunday for the last 17 years. She loves the Lord with all her heart, but she is still being delivered of swearing. If you get on her bad side she will not curse you out but "cuss" you out and then bless you. She reaches out her hands to greet us with a big southern Mississippi hug. Her hands reveal her journey from the cotton field to freedom. The wrinkles and roughness of her skin boasts of the tenacity within. One could only begin to imagine the struggle and the endurance that those hands have gone through. By the muscle of her hug and handshake you would think that a strong lioness roar would be her tone. However, a sweet, squeaky, and delicate voice begins to speak

"Hey sugar, you here for the celebration?"

"Yes ma'am." I responded.

"Well hurry up in here we ain't got that much time."

Ms. Estelle looks down the street to make sure her surprise for Big Lou has not been ruined. She closes the door and leads us down the dark stairway where everyone is at.

"It's not him everyone. It's a false alarm."

She announces while flicking back on the lights. This is my first time in Big Lou's house. Ms. Estelle house is filled with antique furnishing but very clean. The light brown wood paneling compliments the nutmeg color carpet. This space feels homely.

As we entered the basement, we immediately felt comfortable due to all the familiar faces from the neighborhood. Trina whispers,

"Well here is what we have been looking for, music and white Tee shirts."

"Yep."

Lil' Joe the neighborhood DJ was playing DJ Khaled All I Do Is Win. Everyone hired him for their baby showers, bachelor parties, and birthday parties. He wasn't that good but the $100 price for service made him great! Trina began to work the room the way a Diva is born to do. She is standing in the center of the room so everyone can see her glitter piped leggings, glossy lips, and freshly relaxed hair. As expected, the crowd eyes began to glean toward her and Trina has her introductions lined up like dominoes. Trina begins to go around the room and speaks to everyone. "Hey Nino." Nino had his whole crew surrounding him like he was Jesus and they were the twelve disciples. They all had white T-shirts on like they were on their way to the baptism pool.

Trina continued, "What up Sherry girl?" Sherry is the neighborhood beautician. If you do not have the $50 for the beauty shop you can sit in her kitchen for $25. "Tony where your brotha at? Tell him I am still waiting for those tickets… he knows what I'm talking about." Tony's brother works for a marketing firm that is always giving him free tickets to concerts, plays, and sports games. After ten minutes of "The Trina Show" and making sure everyone had seen her famous Friday outfit, everyone is saved by Ms. Estelle announcement.

"He's coming! Everyone shut off the lights, turn down the music, and close your mouth." Ms. Estelle did not have to repeat herself. Suddenly the windows began to rattle from the $700 worth of stereo equipment in the trunk of Big Lou's car.

Everyone said in wave of echoes "It's him!" Big Lou drives a brown four door 1985 Chevy Caprice. It has a couple of rust spots but he always keeps a car wash and in his trunk, he has six twelve by nine Alpine speakers to make the base go boom! This is the perfect car to hold his 6'3" body frame. He weighs around 250 pounds and never had beef with anyone. He is a real cool dude and it shows by all the people who are here at his party. He has rival gang members in his basement who forgot about their beef for one day to celebrate him. From time to time Nino and rival gang member Lil' Mike have turf wars about territories and boundaries within the neighborhood. Last I checked, the street sign said Main St. but they were both determined to be the king of it.

Trina and I prepare to scream surprise on Big Lou's entrance. Ms. Estelle leaves to open the door and lure him down the stairs. We all hear her cunningness, "Hey son how was work today?"

Big Lou responds, "Fine Ma, you know how it goes another day equals another dollar, right?"

"Son I hate to bother you, but I heard some rambling in the basement earlier; can you go make sure an alley cat didn't get pass you when you took the garbage out earlier?" Ms. Estelle ask while opening the basement door.

"Sure Ma, it is never a bother doing something for you." said Big Lou while walking down the stairs and feeling for the light switch. As their footsteps became louder and louder I look around at everyone hiding behind chairs and tables and then at Trina with anticipation and then we scream… "SURPRISE!!!" As the light turns on Big Lou has one fist up to defend his life and one arm in front of Ms. Estelle for protection. He suddenly began to recognize his friends' friendly faces behind his 55-inch Plasma T. V. stand, couch, and hanging out the closet. He realizes what his mom has done. He put his hands up to his mouth and says "Y'all wrong for this… I should have known something was fishy when mom was scared of a cat. That's unheard of. We're talking about a lady who was ready to fight the whole PTA when they wanted me to cut my braids in order to join the football team in junior high." The whole basement erodes in laughter because we know Ms. Estelle is cray cray (crazy) about her Big Lou. He is her pride and joy. When Lou smiles one gold tooth sparkled purposely representing his southern lineage.

"Son, I just wanted to celebrate your promotion on the job and encourage you to keep making your mother proud. Now before I start crying let's celebrate or party as you cool folks say." Ms. Estelle said in a crackling voice. Lil' Joe does not miss a beat and start banging Lil' John.

Trina and I decided to settle in a corner where the new Sears washer and dryer unit was. It is Pacific Blue and has a very modern look to it.   The stickers are fresh on the side of the washer with $499.69 on it. Trina looked around and then asked, "Where is the food?"

You would have thought Ms. Estelle was psychic because she takes ownership of the floor and says, "Excuse me everyone, the caterer just called to inform me he's running a little behind. He should be here in ten to twenty minutes. Here are some bowls of popcorn to hold you until then. I apologize about the delay."

Ten minutes later the doorbell rang. I poked Trina in the side and steered her attention to the finest thing created since slice bread.

"Trina, who is that tall glass of chocolate milk walking through the door?"

"Ken, I don't know maybe he is a cousin of Big Lou or Trina whispered. This guy walks over to Ms. Estelle and gives her a piece of paper resembling a receipt and she nods. A few moments later he comes back in with a case of water, pop, and juice.

"Trina, it is the caterer. I'm going to see if he needs any help with the food."

"Nah you going to see if he needs a girlfriend." Trina said jokingly while my hands wave to shut her up before anyone heard her or she alerted the other girls in the room of this rare find. Sprinting across the room I pray to the good Lord that my spearmint gum has refreshed my breath. Lil' Mike and his crew are playing spades. He tries to catch a quick feel on my butt, but I am two steps ahead of his weak game and quickly maneuver to the left. He looks confused when he misses my butt, stupid little punk.

"Excuse me, can you use an extra set of hands?" I asked to the new face on the scene.

"Sure. My mom owns the catering company so less employees means more profit if you know what I mean. My name is Robert," he said while extending his hand.

"My name is Kendra. I can help you with the table settings."

His handshake is very firm and confident. It stirs up curiosity in me.

"Thanks, that's really nice of you" he proceeds to lay two big aluminum pans on the table which had the contents of catfish and spaghetti.

"Spaghetti and fish, my Ma always told me not to eat everyone's spaghetti." I said trying to make conversation.

"Well mine's always told me no one can turn down her spaghetti. It's one of our bestsellers, but I've heard your saying as well. I can assure you there are no love potions or curses inside this pan."

I lift my fingers and cross them and we both erode in laughter. Right about now a love potion would be alright, I'm just saying. Robert hands me a bag that contains white plastic spoons, forks, and knives. After setting up the plastic silver ware on the tables it is time for Trina and I to play in the Spades Tournament. We are playing against Lil' Mike and Theo who is not good in math so we keep it simple, the best three out of five rounds. We have been partners since the sixth grade. Spades is our favorite game and not too many players can beat us when we play together.

"Trina, you will not believe what's on the menu tonight."

"What, chicken?"

"No, fish and spaghetti."

"Do the spaghetti look safe?"

"Yes, Robert says his mom made it and no one can turn it down."

After the food was set on the table properly, Robert took one more glance over the food layout to make sure everything on the order sheet had been filled. He connects eye contact with me, smiles, and wave good-bye. Ms. Estelle walks in the middle of the room and ask for the music to be turned down for a moment.

"Can we all bow our heads for prayer? Hats off please. Heavenly Father, thank you for this food that is before us. I ask that you bless the cooks and those who have none to eat. Give us nutrition for our spirits and our bodies and we will forever be grateful in Jesus name, Amen."

Ms. Estelle prepares Big Lou's plate first then announces for everyone to help themselves.

Trina looks at me and ask "Well what happened? Did you get the digits?"

"No". Regretfully I respond.

"See if he has any business cards or flyers that way you have a way to see him again without seeming too pushy or aggressive."

Trina is always good at situations like this. As I walk out the front door looking to the left and then to the right there was no Robert in sight. I knew it. Thinking to myself, he probably was too fine for me anyways. Another one lost. Taking a glimpse at the sky, I could only wish it would have turned out better. In my right peripheral a white headlight comes on and pulls in the streets. It's him! Instinctively I flag him down by waving my hands and smiling. The car stops right in front of me.

"Hey, my mom's birthday is approaching, do you have any flyers or business cards?"

"Yes, I do. I forgot to leave some on the table." Robert said while going into his black leather work folder.

"Do you like Peach Cobbler?"

"It's my favorite dessert." I couldn't help but notice his insurance card and peppermint chewing gum in the glove department.

" Well, I would like to make you one for being so nice and helpful. If you write your address down I will bring you one next Sunday."

While writing my name on the small yellow memo pad with a black pen I'm praying that Ashton Kutcher don't jump out of Big Lou's bushes.

"That would be great! It's perfect. That's actually my mom's birthday, June 27th."

It took everything out of me not to include my email & DOB. Do not be desperate is in the top ten commandments of being a Diva.

"I'll see you soon."

Backing away from the car due to a loud horn coming from a raggedy two door cotton candy blue Chevy Malibu that pulls up behind Robert is making the moment bitter sweet. Every young male in the hood has one or has had one of these model vehicles in our neighborhood because it holds around six people comfortably. Robert hands me several fliers to pass out at the party. I toss all but one in the black plastic garbage can behind Big Lou's house. No one is gonna call him before I do.

Happily, I return to the party and show Trina the business card. She winks at me as a sign of approval. Everyone is enjoying themselves and the food at Big Lou's party. I'm sure it will be the hot topic of the block for weeks to come.

Chicago III

The Land of Family

"Good morning Kendra how are you doing this morning?"

"I'm fine Ma."

"I have some breakfast prepared for you. I made your favorite…grits and scrambled eggs with cheddar cheese."

"Ma, I have a surprise for you on tomorrow for your birthday."

"Now Kendra don't be making a big ado around here, having you as my daughter and getting that high school diploma without a baby is all the birthday present I need." .

"Ma do not worry. It's not that expensive and even if it was you are worth every penny."

"Kendra, Thirsty Ted, I mean Ted, gave me an invitation for a get together at Big Lou's this month but I misplaced it. You might want to go visit Ms. Estelle and see when the actual date is. I think it is a surprise so don't ask Big Lou about it."

"Don't worry ma, the celebration was last week and me and Trina went already."

"Was you on your best behavior?"

"Yes Ma'am".

"Good, Big Lou is a great kid. Glad you didn't miss it. I hate to admit it, but my memory is leaving me like a midnight train to Georgia. Today I feel lucky. My hand been itching all morning. Mable and I are going to bingo. I'll be gone until 6:00p.m. The macaroni and chicken are already seasoned and in the refrigerator for later. Put the two pans in the oven on 350 degrees when you get hungry. Kendra do you hear me?"

"Yes Ma'am."

Ma jolted out of a day dream about Robert's brown skin and beautiful smile by her stern voice.

"Don't burn the house down. Turn off the stove when you take out the food and don't open my door for no one, not even Jesus Christ because he knows how to walk through walls." Mama been quoting that line since I was 13. That was her way of saying do not open the door for no reason but a fire.

"Bye Sweetie."

"Bye Ma."

I liked having Saturdays to myself. Today HG TV has a marathon coming on and I am going to pick out the kitchen back drop for my apartment. I'm not moving out yet but that seem like the natural thing to do after graduation. It's great being out of high school. No more going over to Granny's for adult supervision. No twenty minutes talks about not answering the door, now they are one minute. Occasionally ma calls from Ms. Mable cell phone but that's just a mother's love. In fact, I hope she wins at Bingo. Last time mama won she came home with a 52-inch plasma HD TV for the family room. Guess who was conveniently waiting to help bring the T.V in? Thirsty Ted. One of the fliers says this week's grand prize is a trip to Montego Bay Jamaica.

Our last trip was to Smokey Mountains, Tennessee. Our family reunion was there in 2002. Aunt Bessie lost the role of reunion planner after that one. The hills were so steep that mama had a panic attack driving on the way to the cabin. My Pa courageously drove for the remainder of the trip. The way he hid his fear was so heroic. He refused to display weakness in front of us. Mama, Krystal, and I had never experienced hills and mountains before. The fear never left us within the five days we were there but the scenery was priceless. Being up in those hills made you feel like you were in God's front room. Some mornings we had prayer. The altitude was so high that the sun seemed eye level. It felt like we had arrived at the Garden of Eden. There were steel locks for the garbage cans so the bears would not come on your front porch and greet you in the morning. Yeah, those were good times. That was the last trip we took as a family and then Pa died shortly after. It was time for a new vacation, new memories, and a new exploration of life. We are overdue.

Looking at my phone I realize that Trina had not called or texted. This is very unusual since it is the weekend. I'ma call her and see what movie we're going to see and which mall we're shopping at today.

"Hello" Trina answered.

"Hey girl, whatcha doing?"

"You wouldn't believe me if I told you."

"Try me."

"I'm on my way to Ohio."

"Ohio"

"Ohio girl. Sasha is going into labor and my ma wants to be there to welcome her first grandbaby. It was a last-minute decision."

Oh, I'm so happy for Sasha. When are you all coming back?

"Probably in a week."

"Well take plenty of pics and send them to me."

"I will."

"Trina, you know tomorrow the catering guy is bringing mama a peach cobbler."

"Oh yeah, it's been a week already time is flying. Are you nervous?"

"Yes, I can't believe he is going to be at my front door. I have been cleaning the house all week."

"Dang girl, he is dropping off cobbler. He is not doing a home appraisal."

"I know…. but I just want everything to be perfect in the back drop. Trina, I cleaned my closet."

"Oh yeah, you tripping. You'll be fine, just look cute, be courteous, and show him your pearly white teeth the good Lord blessed you with. Alright I gotta go I will call you after the delivery.

"Bye girl."

"Bye Ken."

Trina is so excited to be an aunt and boasts constantly on how she is going to give her niece her very first lip gloss application and glittery diaper bag. Imagine that, newborn shimmery lip gloss! I am friendless this weekend and it sucks. I wonder what Robert is doing. Is he making a catering stop or preparing my peach cobbler? When he smiles his dimples come out of hiding and greets you. If the peach cobbler turns out to be delicious that will be a double bonus. Maybe I will clean all of my gym shoe soles to take my mind off of his smooth, acne free, dark skin, or his perfectly cut wavy hair, and don't even migrate south to those chiseled lips that were created by Picasso himself. His mom must have put Vaseline on his face every day when he was a child because his skin glows with care. See I am doing it again…. somebody help me. I can't stop thinking about him. Maybe it's the fact that he is not from the neighborhood, has a job, and most importantly has access to a car with insurance. These are qualities that any lady would admire young or old.

The truth is my last boyfriend was a jerk. His name was Warren Townsend. Mama did not know about him and I kind of think that is why it didn't work out. Nahhh ..he was just a plain loser, but I still needed mama's blessing. He broke up with me last summer of 2009 through text because I told him I wanted to wait until I get married to have sex and he tested my declaration. We discussed my goals about sex while riding the Chicago Transit Authority (CTA) to Millennium Park to attend the Taste of Chicago fest last year. For some odd reason Warren thought that buying me two books of tickets priced at $8 each would secure him a space in between my thighs. After eating the biggest barbecue turkey legs I have ever seen and tasting alligator burgers our quest was over. Walking home Warren invited me to his aunt Roby house for more barbecue. His aunt Roby was one more sip away from being drunk. She welcomed us with a loud hello and then tripped over her shadow.

"Hello, howz everybody doing?"

I thought to myself "everybody"? It's just me and Warren and he is your nephew. Out of respect we both responded, "Fine."

She immediately asked Warren to go to the basement and refill the blue cooler with water, pop, and beer. Warren invited me in the basement to help him get more pop. Aunt Roby basement was not as well kept as Mrs. Estelle's. There was dirty unfinished laundry everywhere. It wasn't even organized between lights, darks, and whites. Old exercise equipment from the 1980's decorated the rest of the space and two free weights were dangerously placed by the end of the stairs. Out of nowhere Warren grabs me instead of the grape, orange, and strawberry pop cans stacked on the side of the dryer. He tries to shove his hand down my shirt, but I was already prepared for defense thanks to Lil' Mike's weak moves to slap my butt every time I walk to the corner store. I grabbed his hand and twisted it until I heard a pop.

"Oh s#!t!"

Warren responded and fell to his knees with his eyes bulging and face frowned. I hopped over the free weights and ran for the door. Aunt Roby tried to stop me to see what was wrong. "Hey, where's every bodiez going?" Unfortunately, her voice faded away in the loud melody of Marvin Gaye track What's Going On and the squeaks of her rusted black chipped painted gate opening.

On my way home my phone begins to buzz and it said on the screen one new text message. When I made it home I opened up the text assuming it was Warren apologizing for being a jerk, treating me like a piece a meat, and taking me to his drunk aunt house. To my surprise this Negro had the nerves to say and I quote, "You twisted my damn wrist. This is not working. I need a woman not a womnun." What is a womnun, I thought to myself looking at the text perplexed? That is not even a word! I am not a nun. I am a woman that wants to wait until I get married before I have sex so I won't end up with a baby by a guy like Warren who thinks $16 is the price of my virginity. Needless to say, Warren hates my guts and had to miss the first quarter of the high school football season due to his injury by yours truly. Anyway, I can't wait until tomorrow to see Robert. Until then I will watch my marathon on HGTV.

Chicago IV

The Land of The Tradition

Sunday, June 27, 2010. It took forever for this day to arrive. Today is the day I see my Robert again. Within one week he has gone from Robert to my Robert, he just doesn't know it yet. Someone call the doctor, I have come down with a little Robertitis. As I step out of my bed to brush my teeth, I look in the mirror and what do I see? A pimple. *The devil is a liar.* Today is not the day for pimples. Where is the toothpaste because my face has to be flawless? As I rub my face with alcohol and apply toothpaste to this bump I can't help but bow down at the toilet hysterically making it my altar. *"Oh Lord I bind the pimple demon in the name of Jesus. Lord I promise not to buy bootleg movies no more if you make this pimple go away ASAP. In the name of Jesus amen.* "I need a miracle and while the Lord is working it out on my cheeks. I'm going to call Trina and get an update on the new Diva added to the family.

Ring, ring, ring,

"Hello"

"Hey Kendra, what are you doing up so early church doesn't start until noon?"

"Robert is coming over with the peach cobbler today and I am tweaking hard. I couldn't sleep last night. I am so excited, anxious, and nervous at the same time. My leg won't stop shaking."

Plopping down on my bed Trina chimes in.

"Well that makes two of us. Can you believe I am an auntie? I have so many fond memories as a child and they were from my aunties. Kendra, I have some big shoes to fill. Aunt Julia and Bobbie took me to beaches, movies, and playgrounds. What if I don't...?"

"Trina you are going to be a great auntie. Just be yourself. I am sure she will be walking in heels by time she is three." Quickly I glance at my closet at all of the shoes Trina persuaded me to buy because they were trendy for the seasons.

"What's her name?"

"Jessica Patrice Johnson. "

"I love that name! JPJ I can see that monogram on scarves, purses, and glitter lip gloss bottles."

"I know right!"

"Did she get any stitches?"

"No stitches or cuts. She has been thanking Jesus all morning. Jessica weighs six pounds and five ounces."

"Tell Sasha I said congrats."

"I will. So what time is Robert coming?"

"I don't know and this morning when I woke up, I looked in the mirror and noticed the biggest pimple on my cheek."

"Did you put toothpaste on it?"

"Yes, and prayed."

"Prayed?" Trina inquired.

"Prayed. Trina, I miss you when are you coming back?

"Well I was going to call you today and tell you that my sister needs a little extra help around the house and wants me to babysit for the summer."

"Did you tell her no because we have plans for the summer?"

"I did and then she offered to pay me four hundred dollars a month. I want to leave but every time I look at baby Jessica dimples and curly hair I get weak. She is so cute and her jaws are so kissable. Kendra, do you know how many shoes I can purchase with $800?"

"Trina that's two months. I have never been away from my you that long. Do not make me wish for high school again."

"You are welcome at my sister's house anytime Kendra. Maybe we can have summer in Ohio. Sasha has plenty of room and there is an outlet mall a few miles away that we can go to every week."

"I'll think about it. I have to put on my clothes for church. I can't have a pimple and puffy eyes from crying when Robert comes. I will talk to you later."

So let me get this straight. I have a pimple on my cheek and my best friend may not be spending the summer in Chicago with me. We have been together for the last six summers. Who will walk to the store with me? Who will protect me when people cross boundaries in conversations or face to face situations? Will I be able to sit on her porch if she is not here? This is too much stress and too early to deal with it. I will table these thoughts for tonight before I go to bed. Now what should I wear?

Today is a perfect day for Levi jeans. They are so comfy but they also accent my curves. These jeans are the only jeans in my closet that gives Trina competition. One day she even admitted that I should have brought two pairs because they made me look like a Diva in denim and that was hard to do. You need extra charisma to wear denim and be a Diva. You have to have the right blazer, shoe, and shirt to glamorize it. Yeah, I will wear these because I need to be pretty but not pulsating with glitter. I just want Robert to notice me.

Wow prayers works! My pimple is shriveled into a tiny speck and my cheeks smell minty; a double bonus. I guess I will go down stairs and wait for the cobbler to arrive. It's Sunday and Mama is playing her gospel music. It is tradition in our house that Sunday is the Lord's Day. Mama makes a soul food dinner every Sunday and the rest of the week it is a combination of sandwiches, soups, and frozen pizzas. Mama sings in the choir in the afternoon service so we don't have to arrive until 12:00 p.m. She also volunteers at the St.

Elizabeth nursing home singing and sitting with the seniors. Mama thinks she is still forty-five. Sometimes I have to remind her that she is sixty- four, well sixty- five today. I hope Robert arrives before we leave. We did not schedule a time. Hopefully his mom sings in the afternoon choir as well and he will drop off the cobbler early.

"Good Morning Mama."

"Good Morning Kendra."

"Happy Birthday Mama!"

"Thank you baby. The Lord has blessed me to live sixty-five years."

"Mama you truly do not look like it. You are beautiful."

"Thanks Kendra. You're wearing jeans today to church?"

"Yes ma'am." Mama looked at me funny because when she was a little girl it was unheard of to wear pants in church. In fact, to this day I have never seen my mother in a pair of pants. During the winter…skirts. At picnics…skirts. Amusement parks…skirts. Bowling…. skirts.

"Mama I'm wearing a nice blazer and dress shoes as well. You know Pastor Jenkins gone freeze us with that new air conditioning unit." Trina taught me how to dress up jeans with the perfect high heel. She said it adds length to your legs.

"You are presentable Kendra. Dresses just make you look so ladylike to me. I guess that outfit will do. I have made some biscuits and bacon for you. That should hold us until service ends at three. "

Mama is what they call saved, sanctified, and filled with the Holy Ghost. This was an old school phrase for Christians who were from a different dispensation of time. My grandmother came from this era. She refuses to wear any kind of jewelry, make-up, or pants. Pastor Ray Jenkins III made it clear to all the parents that this new generation needed a little more grace and we could wear pants to church. He just wanted us to get there and he believed that God would handle the rest. He has purchased a new air conditioner in church and vowed to never use paper fans again. Church and the movies are the only two places I have to dress like it is winter all year round. I can truly say I see where the tithes go from the church members. Our church has a basketball league, young women etiquette classes, and other resources for the youth and young adults. Mrs. Jackson needed a thousand dollars for her rent last month and I overheard mama telling Sister Claire that Pastor gave it to her. Everyone hugs you and smiles. The walls are freshly painted every two years. There is lotion and body sprays from Victoria Secret in the bathrooms and air fresheners. We have classes that teach us how to grow spiritually and professionally. I am currently learning how to self-publish a book. I have so many poems in my Nike shoe boxes in my closet. Trina thinks there are shoes in them and mama too. It was me and Pa's little secret.

My eyes keep watching the red LED lights displaying 10:45a.m. on the stove across from the table. It is so bright due to the layer of grease I cleaned off of it this week. Mama asked me why I been cleaning so much. I told her I was filling time since Trina was gone. I know it is a sin to worry, but I can't help but to be tormented thinking crazy thoughts. Will Robert show this morning, or will I miss his delivery? We have to leave by 11:15 a.m. to land a park in the church parking lot.

Chicago V

The Land of Introductions

Ding Dong

"Who is this at my door this early?" Mama is looking at me with curiosity. I can't move or speak so I'ma just watch. Mama mute the T.V, walk to the door, and look through the small circle peep hole. I knew it was Robert, but I acted oblivious to the situation. Mama looks at me with a surprise look and then her focus quickly shifts back to the foreigner at the door.

"May I help you?"

"Yes ma'am is Kendra available? I mean Maybeline's catering services." I felt so bad for Robert. He sounds so happy and is unaware of the hurricane of fury that's waiting for him on the other side of the door.

"Kendra there is a young man at the door requesting you. Please explain to me what is going on?" Mama turns around and looks like she is ready to head to the room to retrieve the nine-millimeter Pa brought her for protection. She has over one hundred hours of practicing at the range under her belt. Ever since my Pa died five years ago mama had little patience with strange men at our front door. She named her gun Mr. Thompson after the salesman who sold it to her ten years ago. She always brags on how smooth and persuasive his sales pitch was. She went in for some pepper spray and came out with a pistol. Two weeks later Mr. Thompson got robbed one night closing the store and moved out the neighborhood. Our neighbor's daughter was raped by a guy pretending to be working for the utility company. After that happened Mama has zero tolerance for strangers at the door or entering the home. Mama loves Jesus but she also exercises her right through the second amendment to bear arms just in case Jesus needs a little assistance.

"Mama it's your birthday present. Calm down." Mama looks confused. Looking through the peek hole I am amazed that even in a 3/4-inch circular diameter Robert is fine.

"Mama may I open the door? He catered Mrs. Estelle's party for Big Lou."

Mama's frown began to soften and she exhaled and replied, "Are you sure you know him?"

"Yes."

"One moment while I get Mr. Thompson just in case." A few moments later mama reemerges with her purse on her shoulder and nods her head for me to open the door cautiously. Mama steps back and straighten her clothes and put her game face on. Her game face was a stern look with squinted eyes and her right hand on her hip that conveys "State your business and state it quick."

"Hello, Kendra, right?"

"Yes, Robert, right?

As if his name has not been chanted one hundred times today already. Trina taught me to always come across as confident but not a know it all. Robert is wearing his catering outfit. Even though his hat is white, big, and floppy he is still cute. His name tag on his shirt says "manager" above it. His pants are black and white checkered and he looks very professional. The dessert is in an aluminum pan that is occupying both hands. He has a smile on his face like he is about to sell us a car or a monthly subscription to a magazine. Lucky for him that is not the case because mama is not buying.

"Here is the Red Velvet Cake that I promised you."

"Red Velvet Cake? I wanted…"

"Just kidding. I have the peach cobbler."

"Ahh ok jokester…"

"Um hum um…," Mama interrupts us.

"Oh, Robert this is my mom Mrs. Denise Springfield."

"Hi ma'am. Nice to meet you. Happy birthday from Maybeline's catering."

It was an awkward moment. Robert gestured to shake Mama's hand but he realized they both were full so, he gives Mama the peach cobbler and put both of his hand together and bowed.

"Thank You. Peach cobbler is one of my favorite desserts,"

Mama takes the Cobbler and walked back to the kitchen to put it up until after church. Her frown is loosening up.

"So, you made it?" I said surprising myself.

"No, my mom makes the food I just deliver?" Robert said rather bashfully."

"I wasn't talking about actually making the peach cobbler. I was talking about the delivery."

"Yeah, I told you I would be here."

And then that awkward moment of ten seconds of silence. Robert was just looking at me smiling and then he began to straighten the wrinkles at the bottom of his uniform jacket. It was now or never so I said,

"I just had a crazy question to ask you. I was wondering if we could hang out sometimes and listen to music…but I don't want to cause trouble if you have a girlfriend."

"Whoa Whoa, take a pause and let me answer the first question. Listening to music together is cool, let's do it, and no it won't cause trouble because I don't have a girlfriend. See now I feel like a punk because you asked first."

"I only asked first because I did not know if I would see you again."

"I just thought a pretty girl like yourself would have a boyfriend." His voice was beginning to rise so I had to inform him to lower his voice by putting my hands up in the air and fanning them in a downward motion. Glancing in back of me I want to make sure Mama did not just hear that wonderful compliment Robert gave me that has me sweating.

"You think I am pretty?" I whispered twirling my hair unconsciously.

"Well actually I think you are beautiful." Beautiful, no one has ever called me that but Pa. I have heard fine, cute, precious, pretty, and nice but only Pa has told me I was beautiful until now. It felt good to hear it again.

"No way, you're just saying that." I said to let him know he did not have to try so hard to impress me.

"Kendra, the dimples don't lie and you are making me blush, so there you have it. Its official, you're beautiful." Robert turns his cheek to me and there is a deep dent in his cheek and a smile to accompany it. His teeth are neon white or maybe it is the turquoise blue gum in his mouth that is intensifying the white enamel. Either way it is another reason added to the Why I am beginning to like Robert list.

"Wow, I did not know I was getting dessert and dimples. That's a bonus." After ten seconds I realized I have too many teeth showing, to be exact thirty-two of them. So I tighten my smile and ask,

"Well, what days do you have off?"

"I usually work seven days a week. It keeps me out of trouble and I really never had a reason for a day off? My mom says that an idle mind is the devil's playground. Does Friday work for you?"

Okay Ken play it off.

"Let me make sure." Pulling out my cell phone I open my calendar and look at the empty screen. "Friday is good. Dessert, dimples, and a date. I guess good things come in D's."

Mama footsteps begin to join the backdrop of sound as we begin to burst out in flirting laughter. Quickly I close the door. I don't want to be embarrassed. She told me I could have a boyfriend when I graduated out of H.S, but I know she has to ease into me dating and especially a courting session on Sunday morning. Robert will just have to understand. Lord please don't let him knock back on this door.

"Kendra, are you still at the door?"

"No ma'am." I said walking away from the door and trying to hold my composure. I just got a date with Robert and I did it all by myself. Trina is going to be so proud of me. I was confident, cute, and communicative. The three C's to being a Diva.

"Are you ready for church Kendra?

"It's 11:30 a.m. already? Sure! I have a lot to be thankful for."

Chicago VI

The Land of Fellowship

Sunday is the day we have delegated to fellowship with other worshippers of Jesus Christ. As a child, church was very fun because mama would buy me pink and yellow ruffled dresses with barrettes to match. I remember playing musical chairs in the church mother's lap. Everyone boasted on how I was the only baby that never cried and how I would praise the Lord right with the best of them. As I turned a teenager, I remember thinking church was the only reason I could not go to Samantha Parker's slumber party on a Saturday night. Sometimes Mama would let me spend a night over my friend's house, but it was embarrassing having your mother wake up the whole house at 6 a.m. in the morning to retrieve her child for church. After a while, the invitations stop coming. Now, church is not that bad or boring. I understand the significance of what Pastor Jenkins is saying. When I was a child, I would write letters to my friends during the whole service. Stupid innocent questions I would ask like, who is cuter Teen Wolf or the Karate Kid …circle one? Michael J. Fox always won.

There is a lot of peer pressure in my age group. Pastor Corey is the youth pastor for Sunday school. He teaches young adults ages

18-25 cool strategies to get the devil off their back and out our mental space. Being eighteen is awkward. You are not a kid but you are not a full adult. You're stuck between independence and a 1:00 a.m. curfew. Being in Bible class with twenty-one-year-old makes me feel like a young adult. Mama always reminds me that God is just a prayer away. Lately I have not been talking to him as much. I'm not mad at God. I just seem to forget about praying throughout day until it is time to go to sleep or something bad happens, like that pimple. Sunday is the only day I prefer to listen to gospel music. It sounds like it was made for a Sunday morning. If I am lucky the radio jockey will have a Winans marathon playing all the hits. As we pull up the purple and gold Faith En Route Fellowship Church sign greets us. I don't know how Pastor Jenkins does it, but he always preaches right to me. At least it seems that way. There is a sea of Cadillac and Lexus automobiles in the parking lot. We have the title to our 1999 Lexus GS300. It is fully loaded. Mama paid it off with some of the life insurance policy from Pa's death. Church attendance is getting stronger. Mrs. Ruby, head of the usher board, leads me to the balcony as Mama goes to the basement to put on her choir robe. She hands me a Faith En Route program which highlight events, the prayer list, and volunteer opportunities. Today's sermon is titled "The Best is yet to Come." The scripture is I Corinthians 2:9 But as it is written, Eye hath not seen, nor ear heard, neither have entered into the heart of man, the things which God hath prepared for them that love him. Mama and I love the Lord. Today I really feel like we are going to be OK, even though Pa is gone to glory. God is going to watch over Mama and I and shower us with blessings.

After the service I was filled with hope and confidence so I went to the bathroom and said a prayer inside the stall. "Lord if I can give you one suggestion, can Robert be part of my best to come? This time I did not kneel on the ground. Mama always told me "you have not because you ask not."

I don't know what it is about the bathroom and prayer but it is me and God's special place.

Now that church is over it is time to call Trina and give her the 411. I hope she is home. Oh wait, let me change these pretty jeans for some sweats. They have served their purpose and now it is time to relax.

Ring, ring.

"Hello."

"Hey friend."

"Hey Trina…I miss you. Tell me you are coming home this weekend."

"I miss you too Kendra. No, I'm not coming home but, I know you holding the block down for me. What's been going on?"

"Well, so far so good. Everyone has been getting along well. There has not been any drama on the block. On my way to the store I look at your porch and wanted to ring your door bell, but then I remembered you are so far away."

"Kendra you can still sit on the porch. You are family."

"I know, but it's awkward sitting on your porch without you. Everyone is beginning to ask about you. I guess they miss the shimmer that you bring to the hood."

"Ken my ma called and said a letter from The Art Institute of California came in the mail."

"Have you opened it?" I interrupted with fear. I know I was becoming selfish but Trina is like the big sister I always wanted.

"No, I told her to wait until I get back. It's probably just them reminding me that I need to report to school on August 12th."

"Trina, everything is changing so fast. That's only 45 days away. Every time I call you I find out that the possibility of us spending the summer together is getting further and further away from reality. We have plans for the summer. The Taste of Chicago started two days ago. We are going to miss the Fourth of July fireworks. Navy Pier has a new speed boat ride and the Drive- In is opening up next week. "

"Ken you are making me feel bad. Let's just plan to get together the last two weeks of July. Why don't you come down here to Ohio?"

"Well it looks like that is the only way I am going to see you."

"Ken my sister's fiancé had a barbecue and his nephew name Justin was checking a Diva out."

"What was Malcom celebrating now?"

"Girl it was his first weekend off in two months so he decided to fire the grill up and invite "The Crew" over."

"Is Justin cute?"

"Girl puppies are cute. He is freaking fine."

"My bad… continue."

"Well I was being the friendly and don't forget pretty host. I offered drinks to all of the guest.   Politely I inquired, "Would anyone like pop, water, or juice? He replied, "I would like to get to know you better……damn you fine."   I replied, "That was not an option sir." Although I was thinking the same. He replied, "Well how do I make that an option or possibility?"

"Kendra, he had me at possibility. A man who uses five syllable words is so attractive"

"Trina you are crazy. You always were a sucker for men with a good vocabulary.   Remember Thomas Simpson said the word "Disproportionality" in math class and you dated him for six months. It looks like cupid has been busy.

"Oh, do tell Ken."

"Well remember the cutie caterer from Big Lou's party? "

"Yeah Rodrick."

"No his name is Robert. Anyway, we have a date this Friday!"

"A date?"

"Yes a date. He brought the peach cobbler for Mama's 65th birthday and I asked him out first. I remembered all of the pep talks we had and I asked him first. Can you believe that Trina?"

"No way!"

"Yes way! He was just too cute and I could not risk not seeing him again. I mean with you way down in Ohio I need someone to chill with besides Mama."

"Ken I am so happy for you. Friday night let's have a recap about our dates. Wow we have dates! Is Friday the first of the month?

"No it is the second. Trina I will send you a text pic of my outfit ok. Tell me if it is a win or a throw it out the

win-dow fit."

"Ok, you know I will."

"Well talk to you Friday, love you, and kiss your baby niece for me."

"Love you too."

As I walked back to my kitchen to grab some cherry Kool-Aid and microwave some lightly buttered popcorn I overhear Mama on the phone, "I will have the rent money next week with the late fees I promise."

Who calls to talk about bills on the Sabbath? Until then, I never wondered how Mama paid the bills or if she ever needed help. Was I selfish or did Mama do such a good job of handling the business that I just assumed we were alright without Pa? Mama turns around and see me and ends the call abruptly, "Thank you and have a bless day."

"Mama is everything OK?"

"Sure baby. Everything is fine. Dinner will be ready in an hour. We are having smothered pork chops and rice."

I knew everything was not OK but Mama would never tell me anyway. She has too much pride and she refuse to let the devil and I know she is worried. Her faith is too strong for that. Every word that comes out of her mouth is positive and full of hope. How could I be so naive? Mama was struggling to pay the bills and I have been day dreaming about Robert. Growing up as a child I don't recall hearing conversations about bills. Pa would sit at the table with his check book and add his signatures to the checks that had been written out by Mama. It never dawn on me that now Mama has to write and sign the checks from her bank account. It was one income now and a significant pay difference from Pa's salary at the steel mill.

It is time to find a job and help pay the bills. Sitting at my desk that my Pa brought me for my 13th birthday I think about what type of job will be suitable for me. He made sure my desk was big enough to last me through college. As a child, I played like it was a stage and I stood on top of it and sang The Stars Spangled Banner to an audience which were my teddy bears and posters of Omarion. I heard if you do what you love it won't seem like a job. I am going to look in the classifieds for a job as an Interior Designer or chef. No luck there, I lack the experience and credentials required in the job qualifications. As a little girl, I would sit in the kitchen with my Grandma Lillie and watch her make all of the greats in Soul Food. Pot roast, fried chicken, beef short ribs, macaroni & cheese, fried okra, caramel cakes, sweet potatoes pie, and the best cream of wheat imagined.

At a very young age I understood that cooking fried chicken was an art and you can listen to the popping of the grease to determine the crunchiness of skin. Grandma Lillie seems to never run out of stories to tell as she made cakes from scratch. Stories of how gas was 25 cents a gallon. She always brag that her and granddad married at sixteen and migrated from Rosedale Mississippi to Chicago for employment. Her Thanksgiving Dressing is so rich in flavor it is a sin not to clean the plate or throw left overs in the garbage. Cooking it only twice a year at Thanksgiving and Christmas makes it rare. It creates an anticipation that could only be satisfied by tasting the mixture of spices and getting full off of the love and pride she pours into it.

Only selected family members inherit the family recipes. It was an honor when I was chosen to carry on the family legacy of recipes at 16. Mama and Grandma sat me down and gave me this brown leather book full of recipes and the dates the dish was created. Granny looked at me and said, "Kendra Latrice Springfield you have been chosen to carry on the Springfield legacy of cooking for and from the soul to heal, restore hope, and cultivate fellowship in our family for generations to come. Always preserve the recipes. This book is given in trust and love. Never share recipes. Be careful who you let in the kitchen while preparing these meals. These are treasures, and you have been chosen to guard the jewels of our family. Our recipes were so authentic, many neighbors and friends from Mama's past still pop up on holidays because they cannot find the taste of the south anymore.

My grandma is my hero. She only has a fourth-grade education but somehow with the grace of God she managed to raise eight children, owned over five cars, brought her a building, and always has money to loan everyone in the family with the educational degrees.

Truth is, Mama makes the best peach cobbler but I wanted to see Robert so bad I asked him to make Mama one. I was glad she did not inform him of this when he was at the door. I would have been busted. One cool point for Mama! All this reminiscing about soul food has me kind of hungry I wonder what type of food Robert is catering today? Oh well, I have some pork chops begging me to eat them. Tomorrow I am going to find me a job.

Chicago VII

The Land of Transition

July 1, 2010, one more day before Robert and I go out on our date. As I played back the conversation in my head, I realized we did not set a time to meet. Where did I put the menu to the restaurant? I know where it is. Mama and I have a special drawer in the kitchen with all of our favorite restaurant menus. If you make it in the drawer it is official that you have good food, we will tell our friends and family to support you, and we will order from you on Friday nights. Every payday Mama and I order take-out food and watch movies on cable. Ahhh there it is…. Maybeline's Greens & Things for the Soul. Great, the number is front and center on the front page. Before I call let me practice my introduction…

"Hi Kendra speaking is Robert available" … no that is too corporate.

"Hello is Robert available?" … OK but boring a little. What if he answers the phone do I say "Hi Robert?" or "Hey Robster… Kendra speaking". This is too complicated. I'm dialing the number and whatever comes out comes out. Here goes nothing….

Ring ring ring

"Maybeline's Greens & Things for the Soul what would you like to feed your soul today?"

"Robert... I mean is Robert available?"

"Who is speaking?"

"Kendra,"

This is his mom, the owner. Was there a problem with your order ma'am?"

"No"

"Oh, well would you like to place an order?

"No"

"Oh OK. Well is this a personal or business matter?

"Personal."

One moment please."

"Robert Earl.... Robert Earl. You have a phone call and make it quick, it is lunch time and deliveries are piling up."

Internally I am cracking up at the name Robert Earl. That name is for old uncles, players, and Grandpa's. Robert Earl sounds like it would belong to an old pimp who wears dress socks and gym shoes....

A Dad's Redemption

"Hello"

"Hi it's Kendra."

"Hi Kendra. What's wrong? Did your mom like the peach cobbler?"

"She loved the cobbler. I was calling because I don't think we sat an official time for our date on tomorrow?"

"Yeah you're right. We didn't. What time works for you?"

"7 p.m. is good."

"OK, I will be there at seven."

"Robert, is this a good number to reach you at?"

"Actually, it isn't. Let me give you another number."

A voice became prevalent in our conversation. It was loud, hoarse, and very rude.

"Robert, I need you to get that delivery out of the door. Please!"

"Kendra, is this your number in the caller ID that starts with 745?" Roberts asked in a rushed tone.

"Yes."

"I will text you my number. I have a delivery. Thanks for calling Kendra see you tomorrow at seven."

Wow that was weird. Note to Kendra do not call Robert during lunch hour at Maybeline's Green & Things for the Soul or you will be interrupted, interviewed, and irritated by Robert's mom. Anyway, I have a date so I must fine something to wear. Oh where is my best friend? Trina would know exactly what to pull out of my closet. First let me check the weather tomorrow on the WGN Chanel 9 news. Tomorrow will be a high of 89 degrees and 63 degrees at night. My menstrual is ending so the timing is perfect. Who wants to go on a first date with a hot guy in the summer on the rag? Maybe this blue and coral maxi dress will be cool or the white one. Sweating is not an option. Even though I don't know what we are doing or where we are going I don't want to sweat. As a matter of fact, I don't even care. As long as Robert is the chaperon I will follow. Trina gave me a Diva checklist for preparing for dates. She swears it is the Diva Bible to glamour. OK, let me see how much work needs to be done.

1. Shave legs …check.
2. Shave arms and underarms…check.
3. Arch Eyebrows…. now that I need to do.
4. Get eight hours of sleep.
5. Mani & Pedi.
6. Try my outfit on tonight to determine if it is a winner.
7. Moisturize my body by taking a hot bath and following it up with shea butter body cream all over.

As I wind down for the night I look for my favorite pillow that my pa and I made in a sewing class.   It is orange, soft, furry, and has little bulging polka dots on it. Pa never had a son. His dreams of teaching his son how to play basketball or how to rebuild a motor were put on hold when I was born.   Mama signed me up for a sewing class when I was eight years old at the park district and the last project required a parent to help you sew a pillow. I chose Pa for the parent to help me. The end result was an imperfect shaped orange pillow, thumbs with needle sores, and a memory with my dad that will last a lifetime. He was the only dad in the class, and he endured the laughter of my peers and the subtle advancements from the single moms. Whenever I begin to miss Pa I grab the pillow. It represents sacrifice, unity, acceptance of imperfection, completion, and love. It encourages me to finish what I start no matter the ridicule or the fear of rejection. I had no clue that besides prayer, this orange pillow was going to be one of my coping mechanisms in my life. Sometimes I swear I smell his cologne and cigar on the pillows. My orange pillow has gotten me through good times like when Trina and I watched Love and Basketball three times in one night and the bad times when Pa died and the closest thing to his touch was my orange pillow. This pillow inspires me to write and calms me down when things get hectic. Where's my pad? I have a poem that just came to me about my date tomorrow.

Extra Extra

Extra Extra read all about it,

My period is gone and I'm so excited.

Extra Extra read all about it,

I can wear white and not try to hide it.

Extra Extra read all about it,

My mood has changed no more pouting.

Extra Extra read all about it,

This has been the longest five days of my life.

Thank God it's over,

I'm so delighted.

Chicago VIII

The Land of Preparation

Finally, Friday is here. It is 11:00 a.m. and Ms. Chu Beauty Kingdom should be open now. Today is my date with Robert and I am so nervous. As I go down the stairs I check the refrigerator to see if Mama needs anything from the corner store. She has diabetes but that doesn't stop her from having a can of Pepsi Cola every now and then. She doesn't know that I have found her stash behind the gallon of milk. As I move it to the left I see that there is already one can sitting idle and chilled to perfection waiting to be secretly devoured.

Mama added me to one of her credit cards to teach me how to budget. She believes independence is sexier than any shade of red lip stick. She has $75 dollars automatically transferred bi-weekly and I have to pay tithes of $7.50 to the church every payday. Mama works at the post office and will be retiring this year. She has been a proud employee for 35 years and have received every type of anniversary gift a job can give an employee. She has a gold watch, pearl earrings, name plates, and has been employee of the month over 10 times during her employment. She has been through four bosses and helped train them all. Every day she wonders if this is the day she is surprised by her co-workers with a retirement party. She had been the event host for many of these events and now it was her turn to sit in the hot seat.

While walking to the nail shop I cringed because Lil' Mike and his crew are on the corner. It is 9:30 in the morning why are they up so early to do nothing? They make doing nothing seem like a career. To add salt to my wound Thirsty Ted is walking on the reverse side of the street. I'm going to pull out my cell phone and pretend to answer a call.... dang too late.

"Hey Kendra," says Thirsty Ted with his hands in a prayer formation.

"Hold on please," I say to the make-believe person on the other line. Hey Ted."

"Good Morning, I just need thirty-two cents that's it. If you can find it in your heart and can spare it I would really appreciate it."

Nobody asked for money the way Thirsty Ted does. He is so polite and sincere how can you say no?

"Here Ted, I only have a quarter in change."

As I search for the quarter that was left in the inside pocket of my purse, I begin my fake phone conversation again.

"Now what time is my appointment?"

As I hand Thirsty Ted the quarter he smiles and say, "That'll work," and walks off.

I can here Lil' Mike loud mouth and ridiculous laugh as I approach the corner. He is the happiest and loudest thug I have ever seen. What is so joyous about standing on a corner for twelve hours a day selling loose cigarettes two for a dollar? Here we go, time to deflect the weak booty slap. Five, four, three, two, one… "What up Kendra, did you miss me?

"Not!" I said looking at his eyes and quickly locking in on his hands as they began to come out of his pockets. I realize this phony conversation on the phone is not working so I put my phone in my back pocket as a second layer of defense from Lil' Mike.

"Well I missed you, are you ready to be my girl yet?" He asked in a confident tone.

"Not yet Lil' Mike. Maybe never I will be ready." I said in my sarcastic customary way.

As I walk pass him I can see his shadow approaching from behind so I quickly turn around and he stops in his tracks.

"Don't touch me or I will have my boyfriend beat your ass."

A load roar of "ohhhh" came from his crew and Lil' Mike looks puzzled. Everyone knew I was single and Warren made sure to tell all the guys I was a virgin in the hood.

"You, have a boyfriend? Lil' Mike said in a confusing tone. Well I bet not see you with him because I will be looking for that ass whopping Ms. Lady."

A Dad's Redemption

As I walk in the Beauty Kingdom I can not help but think, what have I done? Robert is not even my man and I have already arranged his first fight on my behalf. Lil' Mike is not going to stop making passes at me and I assured him that the boyfriend I don't have was gone kick his ass.

"How may we help you?" A man said to me with a mask on his face to protect him from the poisonous mist coming from the acrylic nails he was applying. Why don't they offer the customer a mask? Just a thought.

"Eyebrows please. Is Ms. Chu available?" I asked.

They don't like it when you have a preference but the truth is everyone knows that Ms. Chu is the best. She has your eyebrows on point for two whole weeks. While texting Trina I am called to the black chair in the back of the beauty shop.

"Hey Kendra, come sit here. I'll be with you in one moment." Ms. Chu says in her squeaky high pitch tone. Ms. Chu really meant just a moment so I have to put my phone away and tell Trina about my Lil' Mike dilemma later.

How do you like today? Ms. Chu asked.

"I want them thin with a high arch. I have a date!"

"Ms. Chu will make you beautiful, tilt head back. You have been gone a very long time. Lots of hair Kendra. No good!" Ms. Chu said tapping me on the shoulder to reprimand me in a friendly manner.

She was right it had been a month since I sat in her chair and my eyebrows displayed my negligence. "Lip too?" Ms. Chu consistently asks.

"No, just eye brow."

I heard if you wax or shave your lip hair it comes back thicker so I only pluck the way Grandma Lillie taught me. It is kind of therapeutic feeling the sting of the pluck. Ms. Chu doesn't know but I have been studying Mandarin Chinese language on you tube. Here goes nothing...

"xie xie... They are perfect." I proclaimed as I gave her a hug and proceeded to the counter to pay for my service. "Oh Kendra who taught you that? I so happy for you. Now I have to watch what I say about you. I mean around you!" Ms. Chu laughs and hugs me again. "Just kidding Kendra you are Ms. Chu favorite customer. Today you make Ms. Chu happy. Eyebrows on Ms. Chu."

As I walked out the door I began to thank God that Lil' Mike and his crew was not out on the corner anymore. I thought to myself, free eyebrows for saying thank you in Mandarin. I am going to learn a whole sentence because I need a Mani & Pedi next week. Robert and I are going to have a great time I can feel it! As I enter the house I wonder if mama remembered that I am going on a date tonight. She hasn't mentioned it much at all or asked me a thousand questions. Let me write her a note just in case she is not here by 6:30 pm tonight.

A Dad's Redemption

Dear Ma,

Don't forget I have a date tonight with Robert from Maybeline's Green &
Things for the Soul. I will miss not having movie night with you this evening but
next Friday we can have a double feature.

Love Kendra

Chicago IX

The Land of Opportunity

"Robert Earl, are you up?" Mrs. Maybeline asked while walking halfway into the room.

"Ma of course I am up." Robert says while reaching for his watch on the nightstand.

"Well I'm on my way to the gym."

"Ma, I don't understand how you wake up at 5 a.m. for the gym every day. Are you conditioning for a marathon or something?"

"Not a marathon son…yo mama trying to find her another man. Besides obesity never was an accessory that I like to wear."

"Yeah, I notice a double chin coming in." Mrs. Maybeline dashes toward the mirror that shared space with awards, obituaries, and business cards.

"Robert it is too early in the morning to be cracking jokes. Come eat breakfast with me before I leave." "I'm not hungry." Robert says lifting his head up.

"Well just let me talk to you a bit before I go. Who was that young lady that called the restaurant yesterday during lunch hour, the busiest time of day?" Asked Mrs. Maybeline while sipping coffee from her brown mug that proclaims Coffee covers a multitude of sin.

"Oh that's Kendra. I met her last week at one of the deliveries. Remember Ms. Estelle's party for her son Big Lou?" Robert responds from the couch in the living room.

"Yeah Ms. Estelle, she sent us a thank you card for the food. What a sweet lady. So why is Kendra calling you?"

Robert looks in the air and then shakes his head and responds, "We have a date."

"We?" Repeats Mrs. Maybeline as she lifts her head from spreading the cream cheese on the bagel.

She stares into the living room without blinking and inquire more from Robert with her eyes.

"Yeah we. She seems like a nice girl ...what?" Roberts rebuts confidently.

"And how did you determine that?" Mrs. Maybeline puts her hand on her hip and waits for Robert response.

"Her eyes are so brown and bright. When she looks at me and smiles it make my dimples come out. She just seems like someone I would love to get to know more about."

Mrs. Maybeline looks at Robert as if he is as helpless as a wet piece of tissue and interrupts, "Well Shakespeare, remember Belinda seemed like a nice girl until she stole your piggy bank out of your room when you went to the bathroom. You had dimples then and a deficit in your bank account. Remember Jacqueline seemed like a nice girl until she cheated on you with your cousin Jeff. You had dimples then too and a damage relationship with your family. Do you still believe they were looking for a lost gym shoe in the closet Robert? Son don't forget the nicest girl in the world, your dad's rehab therapist Emily who I paid $75 an hour to restore your father's knee and she left with my money and my man in her arms. I know all about nice looking girls and dimples poppin out, so Ms. Kesha..."

"Kendra." Robert corrects.

"Oh excuse me, Ms. Kendra needs to call your cell phone and don't use the business number unless she wants to order some greens and things. What time is this date anyway? Today is the second of the month and it is our busiest day...."

"It is at seven and our last delivery is at 5 p.m."

"Well it seems like you have it all figured out. Just make sure you are careful. These street girls are slick and trifling."

"Mama I told you she is not like that...chill."

Robert walks over to the refrigerator and pulls out the cream cheese to spread on his toasted plain bagel.

"Ma, I think I want to start looking for an apartment."

"For what Robert? This big old house. We have five bedrooms, this ain't enough room for you? I'm barely here, don't I give you your privacy?"

"Yeah, but I'm twenty years old. I'm a man and I should have my own space."

"Look Robert if you want to waste money and go rent you an apartment then help yourself. Staying with your mother does not affect your manhood. I have always taken care of you and never have I ever displayed disgust or dissatisfaction. Everything you have asked me for I have given you. When you wanted to take Karate lessons in junior high, did I not find the best teacher in the whole zip code to train you? When you wanted to meet Michael Jordan did I not send you to his basketball camp? Present day, did I not deposit twenty thousand dollars in your savings account after graduating from college to help you reach your goal of having a million dollars by time you turn 25 years of age? Did I not offer to share with you the business 50/50? You pay bills, you cook, you help, love, respect your mama, and you clean up behind yourself. To me, that's what makes you a man."

"Just forget I mentioned it ma." Robert said hoping to quiet his mom's voice. It was too early for a serious conversation like this.

"I'm going to the health club, Robert. Make sure you set the alarm when you leave. Mr. Castino said his garage door was open last week and he was a hundred percent sure that he locked it. See you at nine sweetie."

"Bye ma."

Robert sits back and folds his arm and rests his head back on the couch. As he rolls the creamy bagel up in his paper towel he rises up to make a free throw shot at the garbage. He misses and cream cheese is smeared on the top of the garbage. Years of house chore discipline prompts him to quickly wipe it up and leave for the opening of the restaurant. He knows that his mom is not use to sharing him with anyone else. Ever since his dad left her for his chiropractor ALL women are sluts according to her. No one ever meet her standards so Robert stop bringing women home or introducing them to her. Either they were too tall, short, skinny, fat, dumb, nerdy, or just plain not the right one.

Maybeline's Greens & Things is a storefront on the Westside of Chicago on Chicago Avenue Street. It's right on the boundary line of Chicago and Oak Park Il. One side is Chicago and trash everywhere and the other side is Oak Park and grass. Mrs. Maybeline owns the whole building. There's an apartment upstairs which is lightly furnished. Robert planned on freshening up after his deliveries in the vacant apartment so he dropped his brown duffle bag by the bed in the back bedroom. Tonight he finally has a reason to trade his chef clothes for his swag apparel that hangs in his closet collecting dust. The apartment is utilized for extra storage for the restaurant stock. While turning the knobs on the commercial ovens to the desired temperatures Robert thought to himself, I am one minute closer to hanging out with Kendra. Robert was determined to make his friendship with Kendra a success. He was going to be in the company of another woman besides his mom and he was looking forward to it.

Mrs. Maybeline's goal has always been to keep Robert busy so he would not become a negative statistic of young African American men of the streets of Chicago. She refused to have her son pumping drugs or babies into the community. She believed the old saying that an idle mind is the devil's playground. She combatted this fear by overlapping Robert's scheduling as a child with recreational and educational agendas. Now as an adult, working seven days a week was normal for Robert. Mrs. Maybeline was building an empire for him. She had big dreams of franchising the restaurant and having Robert as the Co-CEO. The only dilemma was, Robert wasn't too fond of the plans. Mrs. Maybeline migrated to Elmhurst, IL as a permanent residence when Robert entered High School. A northwest suburb that had a great culture of community. She demanded that he played one sport and instrument. Robert chose Hockey for the sport and for the instrument he selected the trumpet. Not having brothers and sisters made Robert feel lonely growing up as a child. He often longed for a sibling to take the pressure and attention off of him from his parents.

As the day passed Robert fought the urge to look at his watch. The thought of being in the presence of Kendra made three more hours seem like three years. Robert packs the four aluminum pans in the customized bags for the last delivery. Most restaurants have certain zip codes they deliver to. Mrs. Maybeline did not believe in turning down money. So she took orders from any customer that placed an order. As Mrs. Maybeline help pack the desserts she can't help herself but to indulge in taunting Robert about his date.

"Do you have enough money for your date?"

"Of course."

"Where are you going?"

"I don't know yet, we are just going to hang and talk."

"Well make sure you open all doors and be on your best behavior. Skanks need love to."

It was useless trying to change his mom's mind so he did not waste his time with a rebuttal. He simply walked to the car with the giant cardboard box filled with the deliveries.

_____#_____

"C'mon not now!" Robert pleaded to the air while banging on the steering wheel. Traffic was becoming congested. As Robert coasted pass the orange vests on the construction workers he was reminded to slow down to 15 miles per hour. Driving 45 miles per hour in a 15-mph construction zone was against the law but Kendra's face was on his mind and he did not realize his feet was getting heavier and heavier on the gas pedal. Suddenly in his rearview mirror he sees flashing blue lights and a blue and white police car. Conveniently an exit was approaching so he signals and merges onto the side. A tall African American officer begins to approach the car.

"License and registration please." Humbly Robert hands the officer the requested documents.

"Here you go sir."

"Do you know why I pulled you over?"

"Well if I had to guess I would say because I was speeding."

"You are absolutely correct. What is the rush?"

"To be honest, I have a date with this beautiful young lady and I was trying to complete my last delivery and beat the rush hour traffic."

"What type of delivery?"

"I work for Mrs. Maybeline Greens & Things."

"I know her. She catered Sargent Nelloms retirement dinner at the Department in May.

"That's my mom." Robert said in a high tone voice feeling a little more optimistic about the results of the stop.

"The chicken was cooked perfectly and the mac and cheese was phenomenal. Let me run a check on your documentation and we'll take it from there. Sit tight."

The police officer double tapped the door and walked away. Robert could see him typing on the micro-computer in his vehicle. He wasn't worried about warrants or violations on his record. He knew Mrs. Maybeline was going to freak out about a speeding ticket especially during business hours. The police officer looks up and begins to exit his vehicle and walk towards Robert in the car while putting on his sunglasses.

"OK Robert, your record is clean so I am going to give you a warning. Slow down and drive carefully. Good luck on your date tonight."

"Thanks sir. I'll send more of that chicken to the department this week."

"What about the Mac?" The officer asked with his arms wide open

"I got you Officer."

Robert raises up the window with a smile on his face.

After the delivery, Robert came back to the restaurant and went upstairs and freshened up. He did not even turn in the receipts for the day because he could not take another comment from Mrs.

Maybeline. On his eighteenth birthday Mrs. Maybeline brought him some Chanel cologne. He has worn it only twice for graduation and a musical concert. He pulls it out of his brown Coach duffle bag and sprays himself up, down, front, and back hoping that Kendra would smell the scent and appreciate the effort. He sits on the couch and pulls his blackberry out of his pocket. As he begins to dial Kendra number sweat beads forms on his forehead. Two rings and a voice answer, "Hello."

"Hi... Kendra?" Robert questioned.

"Yes, Robert?" Kendra confirmed.

"Yeah are you ready for me to slide through and pick you up?"

"Yeah but my ma said she has to meet you and take down your license plate number. I feel like a child, but my Mama don't play when it comes to her daughters. I am so embarrassed and I understand if you want to cancel."

"No it's cool I have an over protective mother myself so I know how drastic they can be. Canceling is the last thing I want to do, I'm on my way be looking out."

"Alright see you soon." Kendra replies with a sigh of relief.

Chicago X

The Land of Love

"**M**ama, are you seriously going to take down his license plate number?" I asked while applying my lip gloss in the bathroom mirror.

"Of course I am Ken. That cobbler was good but not that good that I will just let him take my baby out on a Friday night without any accountability."

"Mama I am eighteen now, I am not a baby."

"You are my baby and always will be."

"But do you know how embarrassing that was to tell him that?"

"If he is not a murderer or psychopath he should not have a problem with it right?" Mama looks at me with her hands open knowing the only correct response would be to *say right.*

Ding dong

"Mama, it's him! Can you please get the door? I don't want to come across as anxious."

"My pleasure, but the way your face just lit up I would say that you are something…excited, elated, or …."

"Mama… go before he thinks no one is home"

Catching my breath I begin to ease drop from the bathroom on Mama drilling Robert with questions.

"Hi young man we meet again."

"Yes ma'am. I brought you a batch of butter cookies from the restaurant today ma'am."

Robert hands her a round aluminum pan with a white paper top.

"That's really sweet of you Robert but are you trying to get me fat? This pan is heavy."

"No ma'am. Its just food is everywhere in the restaurant and I wanted to share."

"So where are you and my Kendra going tonight?" Ma puts the cookies on the dining table resisting the butter and vanilla extract aroma coming from the pan.

"Well actually ma'am we really have not decided on a specific destination but I can assure you she will be safe with me." Robert said scratching his head.

"Young man haven't you heard a man without a plan is a man who plans to fail. Are you a failure?"

"No ma'am…"

"I can assure you Robert if anything happens to Kendra I will be a thorn in your side." By this time Mama was pointing her fingers at Robert.

"Kendra advised me that you wanted to take down my license plate number so I took a picture of it and can text you the pic now if you give me your cell number. Also, here is my driver license ma'am and you can write down the number if that will ease your concern."

"My Robert, I must say you are quite the gentlemen. Thank you for that information. I see you were born in 1989. So you are twenty years old?" Mama was looking at the DL's expiration date.

"I will be twenty-one on November seventeenth ma'am." Mama was looking in the air counting the difference between me and Robert's age.

"Alright I will stop harassing. You can go on a date with my daughter. Two years is not that big of a gap." Abruptly Mama claps her hands once and began to call me..." KENDRA Robert is waiting for you."

Suddenly Mama's mind had changed and she was excited about me and Robert's date. Fear is prohibiting me from looking into his eyes. The floor is my focal point and the tiles guide me to Robert. Blue canvas Levi's shoes, muscular calves, and blue cargo shorts is all I can see and it is enough to give me courage to do a full body glance and notice how color coordinated Robert is. If Trina was present she would have called him a metrosexual. His hair lining is razor sharp. A sparkling glare came from his left ear which has a diamond stub. His sclera is white as snow as if he has never been deprived of sleep.

His lips are brown and full and he gives me a quick smile which highlights his pearly white teeth. His skin is dark and shiny as if he has just moisturized. He is fine and the funny thing about it is, I don't even think he realizes it. The smell of butter cookies and male cologne is in the air. Robert eyes begin to open wider as I draw near. His dimples welcome me and I begin to blush. His clothes appear to be wrinkle free but he is pulling at them and picking invisible lent balls. Maybe he is trying to tell me my clothes are disfigured. So I mirror him and do a smooth seam check down the side of my waist. The seam lines are perpendicular to my hips. Fate would have it that we match. The blues we are wearing are in sync. I hope he likes my hair. It was straight at Big Lou's but after watching the Black Soul Cinema marathon I was inspired to go natural. Tonight is going to be perfect I can feel it. My period bulge is gone. The only thing poking out is where the good Lord blessed me with a little extra cushion on my backside.

"Hello Robert, were you in my closet last night?"

Mama begins to blush and walk towards the kitchen.

"What does that mean?"

"It means we are matching and you were in my closet last night." I giggled.

"Kendra, that dress is almost as beautiful as you. Your hair is all done up maybe I should have chosen something else to wear."

"Thank you Robert, you look like you are ready for the GQ cover yourself. You're fine. Plus the woman should look better than the man right?"

"Yeah, you're right. You are definitely making me look like "the man" tonight."

"You ready to go?" I asked, ready to get the night started.

"Sure." Robert replied holding out his arm.

"Well lead the way."

As I wrapped my arms around Robert mama had a smile on her face which was weird and if I am not mistaken her eyes look watery. Walking pass the kitchen table I blow a kiss to Mama as we walked out the door. My curfew is one in the morning so time is of the essence. Finally we were all alone just me and him. My heart is beating so fast. Robert reaches for the door handle on the car. Wow, a gentleman. The door to his car opens and I enter first.

"Thank you."

"No problem."

The green pine tree air fresher is competing with the aroma of fried chicken.

"Ah look at you being all safe putting on your seat belt and checking your mirrors before we pull off." I tease but really appreciating the action.

"Better safe than sorry right? Besides, did you see your mother's face when she was talking? Are you sure she is not a police officer? Nothing is going to happen to you tonight….. not on my watch."

"Yeah I should have warned you about Mama. She can sometimes come off too strong."

"So where would you like to go Ms. Kendra?"

I wanted to say as long as we are together I don't care but Trina would kill me for that response so I said, "It's up to you. Are there any movies out that you want to see?"

"To be honest my work load is heavy so I don't keep up with the cinema scene."

"Well what do you keep up with?" "Good question. My life is the restaurant, music, and sports."

"Music, I like music. Fantasia is my favorite artist."

"Yeah she can sing and she is very versatile but I listen to jazz music. Usually it's instrumental music."

"My dad before he died use to play Jazz. He would play Duke Ellington and Myles Davis while he got ready for work."

"I'm sorry for your loss Kendra. Myles and The Duke are my favorite musicians. They inspired me to start playing the trumpet."

"I don't believe you. Play me a song."

A Dad's Redemption

In a Sentimental Mood by Duke Ellington and John Coltrane begins to play in disc three. Robert turns it up and signal left to enter the highway going east to downtown Chicago.

"Are you serious right now? This was my daddy song!"

"Uhn Uhn. No way."

"Yes Way!"

As I lay back on the dark blue cloth seats I close my eyes and reminisce. It is rude to talk while it is playing. We both looked ahead in deep thought until the end.   After the song went off I was eager to learn more about this chocolate mystery of a man sitting across from me so I inquired, "What type of sports do you play?"

Robert begins to laugh and put his head down as if he is embarrassed. "Hockey."

"Hockey! I never met a black hockey player…. interesting. Are there any professional African American hockey players?"

"Sure, you have Ray Emery, Evander Kane, and Trevon Daley to name a few."

"I don't know who those guys are but it's still exciting to find out that we are representing on the ice. What position do you play?"

"Goaltender."

"OK, OK. How do you play hockey in the summer?"

"Well I am a member of the Hockey Foundation and we practice in an indoor arena where the professional hockey players practice."

"Wow that is really exciting. I have never been ice skating."

"I practice every Tuesday at 7 p.m. Drop in anytime at the Ice Flounder Arena to watch practice. They also have open skate hours for the public."

"Look at your face it is all lit up." Robert eyes were big and his smile reflected his passion for the sport.

"To be honest Kendra Hockey helped me to cope when my parents got a divorce. I was on the team in Morehouse College and my coach even thought I was good enough to be a professional."

"So what happened?"

"Maybeline's Greens & Things happened. My mother would not accept no for an answer when she approached me to help her with the restaurant. In Atlanta I was somebody, now I am just her delivery boy but she swears I am her partner."

"Wow, I'm sorry. It sounds like you want to be away from her. A scholarship was awarded to me for Chorus at Eastern University. Being away from my mother is unthinkable. We have never been away from each other longer than a week. I don't know if I can go away for months at a time. It's been only me and her since my Pa died. Who will look after her? Who will rub her feet at night?"

"Kendra take it from me, parents are stronger than you think. She will manage and isn't Eastern only two hours away? You can always drive home on the weekends and be with her but college is something you should experience, especially since you have been awarded a scholarship."

"Yeah you're right, I guess I have to adjust to this new season of my life."

More Duke Ellington and John Coltrane was in the air. The music was so catharsis we became silent as we approached the Gold Coast of Chicago. I felt like my dad was sitting in the back seat. I had not heard those songs in six years. As we arrived at the beach the sun had set and the weather was perfect.

"Is this OK?" Robert asked.

"Sure I have not been to the beach all year. I actually forgot how amazing it is down here."

Robert hands swallows my hands. They are perfect. Not too soft or hard. Robert takes his shirt off and offers it to me to sit on top of it in the sand. Mama taught me it is rude to stare but his strong arms and his hairless expanded chest is so muscular, smooth, and tattoo free. Did he ever fall as a child? His stomach is ripped with lines to mark the sets of crunches and sit ups. His navel is perfect. Subconsciously, I became an omphaloskepsis. Weirdly he doesn't seem to know how hot he is. He isn't cocky. He isn't flexing. He is chill and that speaks volume.

"Let's get our feet wet!" I exclaim.

"Woman you trying to strip me? You already have me out my shirt, now you want my shoes too?"

As we are laughing and mildly splashing water a group of females invade our space. Their marijuana smells cheap and they are inconsiderately staring at Robert's chest. It is too many of them to say something, five to be exact, and besides Robert is not my man. There loud banter is interrupting my date...

"Jackie you are crazy girl, why are you trying to do a cartwheel in the middle of the sand?" Yelled one chick who has on a two-piece bikini and white shorts.

"Jackie look at this." one girl pleaded as she did the centipede on the sand. The other girl concluded, "That's a classic...for real."

"Is it me or is Jackie the leader of the group?" I whisper to Robert. Robert smiles in agreement and drops his head in embarrassment for the girls.

"You ready Kendra?" Robert reaches for my hand not impressed with the "Jackie show".

"Yeah let's go get something to eat." I suggest while standing up and shaking the sand off his shirt.

"What do you have a taste for?"

"I don't know, surprise me."

As we go back to the car Jackie and her crew begins to taunt us.

"Aww did we spoil the party? Don't leave we are not done starring at your man's chest." Yelled another girl.

Robert put his arm around my waist and we continued to the car. By the time we hit 31st street I knew where we were going. It was so Chicago of him to arrive at this particular pizzeria. Home Run Inn one of the best pizza distributors in Chicago.

"Are we going to Home Run In?"

"And you know these things." Robert says while pulling in the parking lot.

"Wow, I haven't been here in years."

"" Me neither Kendra. I guess we both need to get out more huh?"

"Yeah it looks that way."

"Is your shirt itchy from the sand?"

"Actually I have another one in my bag in the back. Can you grab it for me?"

Reaching in the brown duffle bag I retrieve another blue shirt for Robert.

"My Mama use to take me here after Friday night church services. That was when she was considered one of the young adults at the church. She and her friends would go bowling and eat pizza every Friday. One day when I was six years old my eyes were bigger than my stomach and mama made me eat all five sausage and cheese slices that I loaded on my plate. I remember being so full that I thought I was going to burst into a big puddle of tomato sauce. Mama, I can't breathe. I cried. With no remorse Mama looked at me and said, "Next time you will remember not to be greedy. Gluttony is a sin Ms. Kendra." Even though I was full for a whole day afterwards, I never lost my love for Home Run Inn pizza. I knew two or three slices was my max."

"Well I will remember that and order a small Lil' greedy."

"Whatever…"

Sitting at the table I noticed Robert has become silent.

"So what types of toppings do you like on your pizza Sir?"

"Are you psychic? I was just about to ask you the same thing. You can't keep beating me to the punch line. I like mushrooms, anchovies, and green peppers"

"No meat?" I asked in amazement.

"Nah, not really."

"I've never seen a guy who works at a soul food restaurant and doesn't eat meat."

"I eat meat but it's not a priority or a necessity especially when you are around it every day. What toppings do you like?" Roberts asks.

"Well I like sausage, pepperoni, spinach, and bacon" My mouth began to water just thinking about the combination of meats mix with cheese, tomato paste, and the dough.

"Wow carnivore."

"Oh you got jokes?"

 "Well let's order half spinach and half sausage."

"Sounds good."

Robert was a gentleman and paid for the pizza and the games.

All night I have watched those luscious lips and dimpled cheeks. Now we are at my door and I am so nervous.   I want to kiss him but I am not making the first move. As we approach my door Robert grabs my hand, "Kendra thank you for a night well needed." He was looking me in my eyes so intense I was taken back a bit.

"I had such a great time with you Kendra and would love to take you out again if you don't mind?"

Don't mind… I don't want to wait was the thought running through my head but my mouth opens and "Sure" comes out.

"May I kiss you?"

While kissing Robert I am trying to remember if I said yes or just open my mouth to speak and he took the lead. Robert tongue is twirling in my mouth round and round. His saliva is sweet and minty from the Double Mint gum he slipped in his mouth on the way to the door. My bottom lip is being sucked and I am melting.

A Dad's Redemption

"Why you stop Kendra, kiss me some more?"

"Someone is coming."

If Ms. Cecil the nosy neighbor sees us I will not get this opportunity again to taste his peppermint saliva. As I begin to say good bye I realize I have his gum in my mouth.

"Do you want your gum back?"

"I will get it on our next date" I smiled and unlocked my door and went in and Robert walked away.

It was twelve thirty and I had made it home before my curfew by thirty minutes. Mama was sleep. She must have really trusted Robert because she was snoring. Immediately I go to the sink and get a glass of water and place the gum in it. It's blue and irregularly round, but it is perfect because it belongs to Robert. Watching the water in the glass prompted me to the toilet. A tingle went through my body and I had to grab the sink to stay mounted to the floor. I have never felt that feeling before but whatever it was Robert was the culprit. That night Robert brought the poet out of me. Tonight the words are begging to embrace paper so I kiss Mama on her forehead goodnight and go back to my room. My orange pillow and black sharpie greets me.

A Kiss Spoke to Me

A kiss told me that your soul has been searching for a home.

A kiss told me you don't want to be alone.

A kiss makes me wish you were here instead of gone.

Come and live within my heart and I promise to keep all trespassers away.

_____#_____

The next day Robert woke up startled by Mrs. Maybeline because she was already sitting at the coffee table at 5:45 a.m. checking her emails. When Robert walked in the kitchen she closed her laptop and said, "Good morning son."

"Good morning ma. What you doing up so early?" Robert asked while making his hot chocolate and pouring it in his blue spill proof cup for the car.

"Well, I just couldn't sleep last night and when I finally dosed off at midnight it was time to wake up again. How was your date last night?" Mrs. Maybeline inquired while peeling a banana that was in the wooden fruit bowl on the kitchen table.

"It was cool. We went to the beach and then had pizza."

"Why you smiling so much?" Mrs. Maybeline agitatedly asked. The banana begins to protrude out of the peel due to the pressure that was being added.

"I'm not. Did that banana do something to you because you are choking the hell out of it?"

"You are doing something to me Robert. I told you that you have to be careful with them city chicks. They are gold diggers and baby breeders."

"Ma everyone in the city is not like that. You should know ma, ain't you from Chicago?" Robert was hoping this question would cause Mrs. Maybeline to reflect on her journey as a Chicagoan and give other women the benefit of the doubt. I mean after all she was successful and not a skank.

"Boy watch your mouth and listen. All I am saying is carefully select your mate. Some girls just want to land a rich baby daddy to take care of them. The restaurant is finally out of the red and there is no room to be sharing the wealth. I've been building this for you for ten years now. Next week I am going to look at some commercial properties to open the second location. Have you thought about my proposal?"

"I told you I don't want to franchise the restaurant. I have other plans for my life ma"

"Like what Robert?"

"I don't know, but not stuck in a kitchen all day or car doing deliveries."

"One date, One, and now you talking and thinking crazy. Your father and I sent you to college to get a degree in business so that we could build a dynasty." Mrs. Maybeline was pointing her finger in unison with the syllables in her words. "How dare you now renege on the plans Robert."

"How can you renege on something you never agreed to? Coach says I am good enough to join a few minor hockey leagues but my availability is what's hurting me. My bachelor's in business management can still be used with the business doing consulting."

"Robert, we did not spend one hundred thousand dollars at Morehouse for you to play hockey, go on one date, fall head over hills, and give us five hours a week for consultation."

"Ma it was a date, that's it…."

"Do you plan on seeing her again?"

"Yeah"

"When?"

"Well I was going to take a day off one day next week."

"Oh Lord. Robert now you need a day off? Fine, what day do you need? It has to be either Tuesday or Thursday that you meet Kesha."

"Kendra ma, Kendra. "I'm leaving to open the restaurant. It's too early for all this, I will see you at nine."

He bends down and kisses Mrs. Maybeline on the right cheek and walks out the door. Mrs. Maybeline gets up and throws her freshly brewed decaf coffee in the sink and walks to her bedroom to prepare for her day shaking her head and holding her heart.

Chicago XI

The Land of Growth

It's the weekend. Mama and I go grocery shopping or to Walmart every other Saturday to restock on toiletries. This week we will miss our customary run due to my Orientation at Eastern University. It is Saturday, July 10 and I have to take a tour of the dorm rooms and make a deposit to secure the scholarship I was awarded in the music department for chorus. I've been singing all my life. Mama says my first two words as a little thumb sucking girl were dada & mama and the rest was lullabies. Mama has boasted to all the church mothers of my college scholarship award. The school is two hundred miles away in Indianapolis which is equivalent to three hours travel time. Trina is going away to Fashion design school in California. Her goal is to become a personal fashion consultant to A-List Celebrities. She could turn the old lady who lived in a shoe into a Diva. She will be returning home in a week. The summer is going fast and we have not done anything on our summer list. Well, we both had on the list to get new boyfriends. Technically Robert and Justin are not our boyfriends yet but they are good potentials. I wonder how Trina's date went with Justin. Mama still has not showed any sign of financial distress but I know what I heard and it sounded like trouble. I need to speak to Trina....

Ring, ring, ring

"Hello"

A dull voice responded, "Hey Kendra."

"Oh know. Let's try this again." I insisted, confused by her tone. "Hello."

"Hey Kendra" Trina repeated in a consistent melancholy tone.

"What's wrong?"

"My sister has called off the wedding, Justin has a girlfriend, and I have five days to send my college deposit in if I am going to stay on campus this fall."

"Trina, why didn't you call me?" I asked while plopping down on my bed and grabbing my orange pillow under my chin.

"Because all the drama happened so quick and on yesterday."

"OK, calm down, your voice is getting squeaky and start from the beginning."

"Justin and I went out on a date to the bowling alley. He picked me up in a gray Maxima, rims and all, and even opened all the doors. Well later on he stopped to get gas. A red four door Toyota Corolla full of chicks pulls up. The cult of girls jumps out and surrounds the car. They were kicking the car and began to yell Justin name and demanded that he come out of the store and unlock the door to get to me.

"What!" I interjected with disbelief.

"Wait, it gets better. Justin finally comes out of the store with cheese Pringles and a lottery scratch off ticket. The shortest girl out the bunch takes her camera phone out and yells, "I got you now. Busted and disgusted.""

"Kendra, she begins to take pictures of us with a cell phone like she is the paparazzi through my rolled-up window."

"No way Trina." I said kicking my legs up and down on the bed.

"Kendra, this negro then had the nerves to walk to their car and describe me to these girls as his cousin from out of town. I could not take it. I rolled down the window and yelled, "Justin must believe in incest because we bump and grind all day in my sister house on a daily. Ken I know you are not supposed to kiss and tell but it just came out.""

"Well there is always an exception to the rule Trina."

"As they jumped backed in the car the ring leader hollered out the window, "Brenda gone kick yo ass Justin.""

Ken, I did not even have to ask who Brenda was. I'm from Chicago game recognized game. I looked at him and said take me home please and that was the end of that. Now it's 2 a.m. in the morning and I come in and take my clothes off and put on my night gown. I go down stairs to get some strawberry Jell-O with the fruit cocktail in it. As I open the refrigerator I feel a slap on my ass that damn near threw me into the potato salad bowl."

"What! Justin broke in your sister house?

"No! My sister husband Stan hit my ass and when I looked back and saw it was him I shut the door and ran to my room. In the morning I told my sister before she went to work at the hospital. My sister went H.A.M. Ken. She woke him up by splashing a picture of ice-cold lemonade out the fridge. That was one of my best batches this summer."

"I can't breathe right now but keep going."

"Sasha screamed, you like to hit people on the ass at the refrigerator? Get out my damn house right now! You ain't even brought no groceries this month and gone hit my sister on the ass at the refrigerator."

"I felt so bad Kendra. I went in the bathroom and grabbed the brown beach towel and cover my mouth and cried. I could hear Stan explanation that he was not use to another woman being in the house and he thought it was her. But that did not make sense to me because he would have just left her in the bed on his way to the fridge. I was hoping my sister would think of this. She did. Now his ass is outside looking in from the curb. Stan and his nephew are history in our life."

"Dang Trina. I feel so bad for you all. That's horrible. I think it is time I come see you. I will have my mom charge the tickets tomorrow."

A Dad's Redemption

"Ken, give it some time. Now things are confusing here and I want to see how my sister is going to handle all of this. Don't feel bad. It's a good thing, better a separation than a divorce. She needs her privacy. I will let you know in a week or two how things are. Until then love you girl and keep me in your prayers."

You could feel the hell Trina was going through in Ohio. So I sacrificed my juicy Robert date story and decided to get on my knees and pray for Trina and her family. I mean she is my BFF and I'm sure we'll discuss it.

As I am talking to God a text comes through on my phone. Is it me or does it seem like every time it is time to pray you either get sleepy or someone calls you on the phone? As I open my eyes Robert name is flashing on the screen. I immediately ended the prayer and grabbed the phone. The text read, "When can I see you again?" I looked in the sky and said, "Lord what should I say?" Oh my goodness, he wants to see me again. We had a great date but I just thought he was too perfect to be mine. Let me take a second to look at the message and make sure I read the text right. It is a request for a date, so I responded Thursday same time.

When me and Mama arrived at Eastern University I was very surprise at how friendly the staff faculty was. They had smiles on their faces and when you asked them questions they actually gave clear responses. This was totally opposite of my High School teachers. They were very unapproachable and robotic. If you had a question you felt stupid for asking. We were instructed to go to Choir Auditions. I was instructed via email to have a solo prepared. I have two songs that I knew I could jam. Fallin by Alicia Keys and

Precious Lord. After hearing some of the other auditions I chose "Fallin". It really brought out my ability to carry my voice, runs, and ranges. Mama embarrassed me by giving me a standing ovation. The dorms are small but very roomy. I hope I can get a cool roommate who is not lactose intolerant. That is all I ask Lord. I'm going to need cookies and milk night to vent sometimes.

After Robert took me on my next date it was official. We went ice skating and Robert held my hand on the ice and taught me how to ice skate. I fell three times and Robert was there to pick me up. My respect level has increased for professional skaters. We are a couple and it is time to learn more about each other. Robert shared that he is allergic to peanuts and he hates mustard. He wishes he could get his parents back together but appreciates the gatherings at sport bars with his father to watch sport events without his Mrs. Maybeline. He chose to live with his mom on that confusing day when he was given an ultimatum to pick a parent to live with. He was 16 and still a mama's boy. Sometimes he wonders how different his life would have been if he would have chosen his dad. They are not divorced but have been separated for five years. Robert senior is not a stern disciplinarian but never had to repeat his self twice when distributing rules. He is a retired nurse in the Army.

Mrs. Maybeline has a surprise birthday party on August eighth. Robert invited me as his guest. While attending the party she introduces me to all of his family as "his friend" instead of girlfriend. At first I was offended but then I realized that is just the way that she is, mean and pettifogging. I should juke him on the floor just to show her and the world that I am more than a friend. Mama told me to never compete with a fool and that is what Mrs. Maybeline is becoming in my site but I would never tell Robert that. At first my Mama had a problem with Robert's age since I was only eighteen, but Robert charm was undeniable and very innocent. Plus in three months I will be nineteen. It is almost like he doesn't know how special he is. The age difference is a bigger turn on. I feel protected when I am with him. I must admit he is smarter than me and I don't mind. He has a black belt in karate and he teaches me lessons from time to time. The next time Lil' Mike tries to hit my booty I am going to try a low block reverse punch. He blushes about my virginity and calls me his jewel because I am rare and special in comparison to his past girlfriends. Even though he has been with women before he never pressures me about sex and that makes me want to give it to him more. But he always cool down the situation by getting up and walking away or telling a corny joke like, "There go your mama" so convincingly that I get up running for dear life.

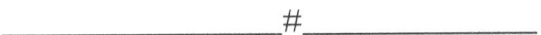

Trina decided to stay in Ohio to help her sister in the transition of losing a fiancé and she became a waitress at Hooters to help with the bills. Since she is not coming home, I decided to visit her. It is August already and this summer without her has been weird and boring. We only have four more weeks before we go to our Universities. I'm surprising her on the job. As I enter the Hooters to my amazement she has blinged out the Hooters logo on her uniform. Now how she persuaded the manager into letting her do that I will never know? She is the only Diva serving wings in shimmer.

"Excuse me, can we have a table for seventeen?" Trina turns around expecting to see who the seventeen people were and begins to jump up and down in excitement.

"Ken! What are you doing here?"

"I couldn't take it. I was missing you girl so I called Sasha and brought a bus ticket."

"Wait, Sasha knew about this?"

"Yep"

"Sasha wrong for that. Do you want wings?"

"Girl of course I want wings. Who comes to Hooters and not order wings? I would like a dozen of mild and buffalo combined."

As Trina walked away to put my order in I pulled my pink jacket out and wrap it around my shoulders. There are a party of six firemen in back of me eating lunch and they all are fine and very loud. I couldn't help but over hear them talking about their wives and girlfriend pet peeves.

"My wife hates it when I burp after drinking beer. She says it smells like bologna." After a roar of laughs another fireman shared.

"My wife said that she hates falling into the toilet in the middle of the night because I leave the seat up. She always screams "Harry, damn you!""

I couldn't help but think about the things that Robert will do that gets under my skin or what I will do that he will tell his friends he hates. Trina appears at the table after fifteen minutes with a platter of wings, shrimps, cheese fries, and a side of ranch dressing.

"Who is paying for all this? I only have ten dollars girl."

"Don't worry about it. It is on the house." Trina said waving her hand to me to put my money back in my purse.

"Trina why are you the only one with diamonds on your uniform?"

"Well, I won employee of the month that came with a $250 bonus. I went to my boss and asked him if I could customize my outfit instead of the bonus to show my distinction and he agreed. And the rest as they say is glittery."

"So did you pay your deposit for school?"

"Girl yes, my deposit is taken care of. I have been saving all of my checks and will be officially moving to California in September."

"I am so proud of you Trina. We are truly growing up."

"Yes we are. Well I have to get back to work. I get off at five. I will see you at the house. How long are you staying for?

"Two days."

"Great. I'll see you at five enjoy them wangs."

The next two days Trina and I shopped, went dancing, and ate chicken wings every day. I left Ohio five pounds heavier but it was worth it.

Chicago XII

The Land of New Beginnings

Walking the river walks with Robert is such a drastic change of scenery from my neighborhood. Instead of manicured grass and flowers for landscaping it is empty cans and potato chip bags. The CTA was our choice of transportation because it made all of the landmarks accessible for cheap. Trina and I are using social media to keep our friendship strong but deep in my heart I know things will never be the same. She was changing before my eyes into a woman. Her look was morphing into a diva 2.0. She looked glamorous at 8:30 in the morning on skype. I still had crust in my eyes and hers were painted with the color scheme of the day. Fashion was her passion. The liberty of sitting on her porch and having the burden of finding out where the party is at was gone. Life has changed and very quickly. It was time to grow up. Our family needed us to become women and that is what we are becoming.

Finally I landed a job at the second-hand store. August 15th they hired me to work as a cashier. Although I have only three more weeks in Chicago, I accepted the position. Every dollar counts. It was an easy move because I was a regular customer and everyone knew me on a first name basis anyway. It was my dream job. I figured I would give my check to Mama as a going away gift. Mama was reluctant to accept money from me but I persuaded her that we were a team and it was my way of showing God that I honor her.

My birthday is approaching soon. December twenty second I say goodbye to being eighteen. I'm over it anyway. As a child I dreamed about getting older to gain freedom and responsibility. First it was turning 13 years old so I could go outside by myself until 10 p.m. at night. Then it was turning 16 years old so I could wear make-up. Then turning 18 years old so I could finally be done with high school and date. But you know what? It is more exciting dreaming about these age milestones than reaching them. Once they come you realize that everything is not what it seems. Staying out until 10 p.m. landed me more mosquito's bites on my arms and legs in the summer. Wearing make-up at 16 years of age made older men look at me creepily. Being eighteen was boring until I met Robert. To be honest I feel like I am a little ambiguous to men. Luckily God gave me a nice and respectable one who does not try to take advantage of my lack of knowledge or experience.

Today is my day off. I am meeting Robert. If Mrs. Maybeline knew we meet in the apartment upstairs she would lose her wig. She wears these human hair wigs that display what mood she is in. She has a long blond one for when she is feeling youthful and considering dating again. When she is mad she wears this short black feather one and black glasses that yells I am on the rag.

Robert and I started meeting up there regularly just to get away from everyone. It is so well furnished I can't believe no one occupies the apartment but the frozen food and fresh produce. Tonight I am meeting him there at nine. We are going to rent some movies and just chill tonight. Before I meet him I need to go to the pharmacy to pick up Mama's prescription. Walmart is crowded as usual. So I skip the urge to peruse the clearance aisle first and stand in the pharmacy line. Mr. Hampton is the head pharmacist on the shift. He has been advising me for the last three years on how to lower Mama's blood pressure with exercise and nutrition. Mama just started taking her medicine consistently. She had been in denial of her medical diagnosis and refuses to ease up on the salt. As I approach the counter Mr. Hampton smiles and says, "Kendra, how are you today?"

"Fine, Mr. Hampton. How are you today?"

"I'm good but I will be better when I go on vacation next week?"

"Oh yeah, where you going on vacation?" I asked assuming he would say Las Vegas or somewhere exciting.

"I'm going to Georgia. I've always wanted to move there so I am going to price some land down there." Mr. Hampton said while double checking the name on the white stapled bag of medicine and handing me the pen to sign.

"Well good for you. Uhm Mr. Hampton there is too much medicine in this bag." I informed him in cheerfulness. Mama did not need more medicine. It was hard enough to get her to even take the prescription now without her feeling convicted in her faith. Jesus was her doctor. As I handed him the bag he checks the computer system and then hands me back the bag, "Kendra, I am certain this is your mom's medicine. I'm not allowed to discuss her medical condition but when she discusses it with you I will be happy to answer any questions you may have. I am sorry Kendra." I grabbed the bag and could not believe that this was so far two secrets Mama has not shared with me. While driving home I can't help but ask God. "What is wrong with Mama Lord? Please Lord tell me, is Mama OK?"

As I enter the house my knees are wobbly and I get dizzy. I run to Mama and fall to the floor in the bedroom. I have already loss papa I can't lose mama.   Mama lifts up my head and say, "Child, what's done got inside of you?"

"Mama, Mr. Hampton told me that you have to tell me why you have more medicine than the last pick up. What's wrong mama?"

"Nothing, Kendra." Mama said while moving my hair out of my mouth and eyes.

"Mama, I need the truth." Mama faith was too strong to claim any sickness or disease so I had to reword the question. "Mama, what does the doctor say is wrong with you?"

She looks at me with squinted eyes and realizes she has been outsmarted. "Mama, let me help you." I said to comfort her and sway her to share her diagnosis.

"Well Kendra, the doctor says that I have glaucoma in my eyes. They say within a year I will be without vision. I was able to hide it from you because of the summer. So when I wear these sun glasses no one knows. Kendra what will I do if I can't see your beautiful face anymore? I need to see you walk down the aisle. I want to see my grandbabies faces?"

"Mama stop crying." She shocked me with her response because I had not even planned that far in my future ...grandbabies? "Mama we are going to continue to pray and believe that God is the great physician and He has the last word, right?" As I stand to wipe her tears she begins to fall to her knees. "Mama, get up mama."

"Kendra I am tired. I need Papa. Why did he have to die?" Mama pounded the floor over and over again until she just rolled over and got in the bed. I rubbed her back until she went to sleep. How can I leave ma at a time like this? I am contemplating not going away to college. Luckily, I put Harper College on my FAFSA as well. It's local and my plan B.

Robert and I have a date in an hour but I am not feeling pretty right. I just want to shower and put on some sweats. This explains why Mama has suddenly begun to let me drive the family car more often. I asked her for a new car but she told me that the car we had was sufficient and begin to be more lenient with it. As I pulled up to the apartment above the restaurant I see the bathroom light on from the left side of the brick building. It is Robert's code to signify that he is upstairs. Robert surprises me by opening the door with flowers on the first knock.

"Wow, are we anxious to see someone?" I say while holding the red roses Robert picked out for me.

"Very." Robert responds.

His soft, full, and loveable lips are going to ruin me one day I just know it! Robert tries to greet me with a kiss but I turn my head.

"Robert, I'm really not feeling well."

"I apologize Kendra, let's go upstairs. Is everything ok?"

Walking up the stairs I don't reply to his question. It is too soon to burden him with my problems. I try to clear my head. Hopefully Robert has some great movies to watch. As I enter the house I smell fresh Murphy oil on the wooden floors. Scents lift my spirit. Stevie Wonder Always is playing in the back ground. As I began to do the whop Robert joins me. Somehow we always get lost in music that most consider is "Old School". Robert looks at me and I brace for him to say something negative about my appearance. I just got through crying with mom and nothing I have on showcases my curves.

"Kendra, you are even fine in sweats…damn."

"Thanks but I don't feel fine. Roberts turns down the radio and leads me to the couch.

"Let's talk about it." As Robert looks at me with concerned eyes tears begin to fall and I land in his strong, muscular, Chanel scented arms.

"Kendra. Kendra, what's wrong?"

"I just found out that my mom has glaucoma and within a year the doctor says she will be blind. It's not fair. I have already lost my pa and now my mama is fading away. I'm sorry I should go."

As I try to get up Roberts hold me tighter and says, "Please, let me help you." The scent of him makes me submit to his plea as he continues to speak. "We will get through this together. I can help you. My mom has a lot of doctors that plays golf with her. Did your mom get a second opinion?"

"I don't know." Robert takes out his wallet and begins to go through his rolodex of business cards and hands me one with a Dr. Cebalis name on it. Call him on Monday and make your mom an appointment. He will give your mom a referral to a specialist in the network. Now stop crying. I can't take seeing the women I love hurt."

"You love me?" I ask while he wipes my tears.

"Yes. I love you Kendra Latrice Springfield."

"You remember my name Robert Earl Thompson?"

"You remember my name, my whole government huh?"

For a moment my tears stop and we laugh.

I can not help myself. I rise up from Robert and sit on his lap facing him and begin to rub the back of his neck and kiss him in a way that I have never kissed anyone before. He grabs my hands and says, "Kendra that is my spot, stop."

Now I have heard about "The Spot" from Trina and I was told not to touch the spot or go to "The Spot" unless I was ready to go to hang out at "The Spot". So I kissed him even harder and begin to rotate my hips. Instantly a protruding bulge came from Robert pants and this time I was not afraid of it. Robert tried to tell a joke, "Mrs. Springfield, how you get in here?" but, it was not funny. I wanted him and I wanted him now. He looked at me and said, "Kendra I am only human. Please stop. I respect you so much and I don't want you to hate me in the morning."

"I won't Robert." I said trying to hold him close.

"You will." He said pulling away. "You said you were saving it for your husband and I don't want to take that from you or from him." He picked me up from his lap and went to the other end of the couch. After two minutes of silence he dims the light and begins to kneel on the floor and start crawling towards me, "Will you marry me one day? I know I don't have a ring but I do have love for you and I am in love with you. So would like to be my wife one day?" I could not believe what Robert was asking me. "Are you sure?" I asked. He looked at me and said, "Will you marry me one day?"

"Yes." Robert gently pushed me back on the couch and slowly climbs on top of me. He looks at me with such endearment and begins to kiss my breast so softly that his lips felt like cotton balls. Nothing existed anymore but me and him. Not my goal of saving my virginity. Not the clearance from Trina. Not the promise I made to God. He kissed the pain away, the anxiety away, and most importantly the curiosity away. He took the black elastic ponytail holder out of my hair and begin to massage my scalp while kissing me and grinding on my pelvis. Slowly I pulled off my sweats and asked him to take my virginity and make me a woman. He looked at me and said,

"You are more than a woman you are a queen, an angel sent from heaven, and my soul mate." He gradually pulled out his penis and gently put it at the opening of my vagina.

"Are you sure Kendra?"

I scooted forward and felt pain and passion at the same time. Every pump he gave me ended with I love you. I love. I love. I love you. I love you. I love you. I love you. We both cried.

As I drive home I can't believe I just had sex. It is August 21, 2010. I can feel my heart beating through my vagina. I just want to go home and lay in my bed. Robert's cologne is all over my body and clothes.

Mama is sleeping and I am glad. If I had to hug her tonight I would be busted. I definitely have something to write about tonight. My orange pillow and pad greet me as I enter my room.

The Cure

I never like the color brown,

Until my eyes were seduced from your dark complexion.

It was reciprocal with the Earth,

The Sun,

The Moon.

Blue,

I wasn't too fond

Of, until you kissed me.

I was catapulted into the sky,

Where God lives.

Red,

Made me think of Blood.

You gave me a dozen of roses,

Now, I think of Love.

Green,

Represents immaturity,

Like the time we played ding dong ditch.

White,

A Dad's Redemption

Well that's too easy.
Remember we stop to have French fries,
They were good,
They were greasy.

Black,
Scares me.
You turned off the lights,
I felt and listened to your heartbeat.
The hues of passion lit up the room,
I wasn't afraid anymore.

Truth Is

Truth is,
God created you for me and me for you.
Wherever life takes me I don't mind.
As long as you are by my side,
I have reached my destiny.

Truth is,
Potpourri may smell sweet,
But it can never compete;
With the scent of your soul,
Manufactured only in heaven.

Truth is,
I've been blessed to love and be loved.
If I never receive a big promotion,
Fit in that little black dress,
Or purchase a grand house,
I have experienced all I need.

Truth is,
I can't imagine life without you.

You make the morning sun shine brighter,

You make water a little wetter.

You bring to a joke more laughter.

You are my birthday gift from God.

When destiny arranged for us to meet,

I became complete.

Reality sunk in after the poetry. I had to face God. It is time to pray and my virginity is gone. I'm mixed with emotions. Robert proclaimed he loves me and that he will marry me one day but today I am not married and I have sinned. As I lay on my orange pillow I begin to pray.

"Lord I am so sorry for the fornication committed. Lord I love Robert but I love you more. Please forgive me and help me to stay on the right path."

The next couple of days Robert and I talked frequently about what happen. I wasn't mad at him but I knew I was moving too fast. College was starting in a few days and I did not want anything to come in between my decision to attend Eastern University. Papa made me promise him that I would go to college and pursue my dreams and goals of becoming the first business owner and college graduate in my family. Now with Mama being sick everything was spinning into a big whirlwind. We did not use protection and now I had to wait for my period to come to breathe again. It is due on the August 29th.

Honestly even though Trina has been missed this summer I realized I have been living in her shadow. I'm beginning to discover myself. I found out that I am a passionate customer service rep. Everyone boasts on my customer service skills at the second-hand store. One customer told my manager Cedrick that I take the shame away from buying used items in just one week. We met in the shoe department.

"Excuse me ma'am, today it is fifty percent off on blue ticket items so those shoes will be $4.99 instead of $9.99 correct?"

"Yes, that is correct."

"Can you try them on for me so I can see if my daughter will be able to fit?"

As I looked around to make sure this customer service deed would not come back to bite me I noticed that my area had low congestion so I agreed to try on the silver Nine West flats with rhinestones on them.

"Wow they fit perfectly what size is this mam?"

"A 9 ½. My Sabrina has been that size since she was thirteen. She seventeen now and I have to shop smart. I got an old shoe box I will put them in and she will never know where they came from. Did you say they will be $4.99 today?"

"That's right."

"For that price I'll buy them and if Sabrina can't fit them I will donate them to the church."

I was hoping she would change her mind on her way to the cash register but she already had her phone out taking pics and texting someone else to get a second opinion. We can only purchase items before our shifts or our off days.

Cedrick congratulated me through email and announced it to the whole team. Truth be told people are fun to be around. You get a chance to hear different opinions and points of views. The things people give away is unthinkable. The art and china are collectibles items and worth thousands of dollars. I have started collecting tea sets. Never had tea and crumpets but I can only imagine feeling royal and sophisticated while sipping slowly and inhaling the steam. Mama has me watching a new series. It is the Antique Road Show. Watching people who spend ten dollars for a $20,000 picture is very exciting. My co-workers call me weird. I can't wait until I have the opportunity to decorate my first place.

Chicago XIII

The Land of Surprises

As I walk into the kitchen I can't believe my eyes. Mama has bacon, grits, scramble eggs with cheddar cheese, salmon crochets, apple juice, and biscuits and syrup on the table and it's not even Sunday.

"Kendra, breakfast is ready."

"What is the big occasion? Did we win the lottery or something mama?"

"No my heavens no. Can you go in the front room and turn down the T.V.?"

"Trina! Trina! Trina!" I scream while jumping up and down. "What are you doing here?" Trina is standing in my front room hiding behind the wall. How did they manage to trick me?

"I can go back if you want me to."

"No. I can't believe you are home oh my God! Let's go to my room."

Mama made me and Trina a plate full of bacon to take to the room and catch up on all that we had missed during the summer.

"So how are you and Robert doing?" Closing the door I am filled with anticipation to tell her about not being a virgin again.

"Trina, I gave Robert some."

"Some what?"

"You know." I said looking at her intensely hoping I did not have to say it explicitly.

"I don't know...wait a minute!" Trina begins to run in circles in the middle of my room. I grab her and pull her down to the bed and shh her before Mama comes in.

"Kendra, I leave for three months and you turn into the couchie houchie. Did you have on a matching bra and panty set?"

"Yes!"

"Was it good?"

"Girl soup is good it was great!"

"Dang!"

"Shhh Shhh!"

Trina looked at me and gave me another hug and said, "Don't feel bad. I gave Justin some too. I know I should not have, but I did. Is Robert a sweater?"

"No! I was so happy that he did not drip on me like you described. My eyes were closed so I don't know if he made ugly faces."

"Trust me, he did. We only have two days before we go away to school. Let's make it count."

Now was the time to tell Trina of my decisions about College. For the second time I have made a major decision in my life without her influence or input. I don't know how she is going to respond but here we go.

"Well, Trina I have decided to stay here with mama and go to Harper Community College."

"Is everything OK? Ken I understand that you have a boyfriend but you going away to college is something I thought you wanted to do. It's practically three days away."

"I do. I mean I did. Mama, has glaucoma really bad and she is losing her sight."

"Ken, I'm so sorry. When did she… How did you …Do you need me to do anything?"

"Just pray for her and me that God works a miracle in her favor. Robert gave me a card to a specialist and I am trying to get her to call but you know how mama is about her doctor. Dr. Wilson has been her doctor for ten years."

"Ken, you put Harper down on your FAFSA as a backup right?"

"Yeah."

"Oh OK. Well you straight then. I don't care what nobody says always keep a plan B."

Our friend Kalen from school let us catch up on all the blockbusters films for the summer at the movie theatre. Trina and I went to the show and paid for one movie but seen three movies that day.   We saw The A Team, The Karate Kid, and The Last Air bender.   We tried to fill in as much fun as two days would allow. We cried and laughed together so much.   After seeing mama breakdown I could not leave her in Chicago alone.   Trina went off to college. I rejected the scholarship to Eastern University and started Harper City College September 6, 2010.

Fall is here. This is an awesome time to take pictures with orange, brown, and red leaves. Robert and I take advantage of the free photo backdrop of nature. I have started a photo album because I can't trust the phones to hold such monumental moments of my life.

My cell phone alerts me according to my period tracker I am late by five days. In the past this would have been a good thing but due to my recent endeavor of Robert making love to me I am disturbed. I went to the drug store and purchased a pregnancy test but could not take it at home. Mama would kill me if she seen that test in the garbage so I am going to McDonald's and take the test there.   While waiting for the results in the fowl smelling bath room I pray that the results are negative. I begin to think only positive thoughts and think of what victory dance I am going to do when I see the minus sign.

Maybe I will go old school and do the cabbage patch or the running man. Maybe I'll be MJ and fake a crossover and make-believe dunk. No, I'm going to be Queen Elizabeth and wave my worries away eloquently. Well I'll be damn…my sins have caught up with me. The room is spinning and I can't seem to land against the wall to catch my balance. I hope this is water on the floor from me washing my hands, but I doubt it.

"Lord I said I was sorry. You know Mama gone kill me. I am going to be the talk of the church. Lord what am I going to do? When mama find out, I'm coming to hang out with you Jesus."

After having a conversation with God I realize today no miracles will be performed on my behalf. I am pregnant. Luckily my black pants hide my soiled pants. My stomach feels nauseas. Is it because of the news I just found out or is my child hungry? Wow, I have a child growing inside of me.

For the next two weeks I did not talk at all to anyone, not Trina, Robert, or Mama. I could not take the embarrassment. All I had was my orange pillow and my sharpie pen to comfort me.

QUESTION?

Am I allowed to make a mistake as a child,

Or will it hunt me like a lion in the wild?

Am I allowed to make a mistake as a child,

Or will you hold it against me like flesh and a blouse?

Am I allowed to make a mistake as a child,

Or will it follow me like a shadow silhouetting my imperfections?

Trina did not deserve to be in college worried about me. Robert left numerous emails and text but they went unanswered. Confusion and fear were setting in. I called my cousin Peyton on Pa side and asked him to loan me two hundred and fifty-seven dollars for an abortion. The law was on my side. At age eighteen abortion can be performed without your parent's consent.

The abortion clinic is very discrete. Driving pass the building you did not know they kill babies in there. Entering, I see so many females of all ages. One girl is as young as twelve. Her mama practically has crackers in a plastic bag for her to be quiet in the doctor's office. Two friends are laughing and dancing as if they are going to try out for "She Got Talent". Embarrassment is all over the mom's faces. Everyone is avoiding eye contact. Some females look sophisticated with pearls and fashion scarves and looked like Liberians. There are no seats available, apparently abortions are trendy. We all have made the same decision to kill our unborn child for whatever reasons. It's a sisterhood of secrecy. There is a fog of deception in the air and we all are carrying ourselves like we are just getting a routine physical.

"Did you sign in?" One of the nurses asks from behind the counter.

"No."

"Please put your name and insurance carrier on the sheet."

"It will be cash"

"Oh, well state that on the sheet please."

As I walked up to the front desk to sign in I ask for the key to the bathroom. The friendly Asian nurse named Jackie hands me this sticky lump of plastic with gray tape and a silver key at the end. She directs me to go down the hall and make a left. The egg yolk yellow painted bathroom immediately stirs my sensation to urine. I lock the door and begin to pull down my pants to pee. While pee is trickling into the water the sound of splashing is interrupted by a baby's gentle voice, "Mama what did I do?" Who said that? I looked around and no one was in the bathroom but me and those piss colored walls. I think to myself you are tripping. Again the voice asks in a loud, gentle, and clear voice, "Mama, what did I do?" It was my baby speaking to me. God had allowed me to meet my child audibly before I killed it. My child wants to live and know what it has done to make me want to end its journey from heaven to earth and into my life. I could not answer the question so frantically I run out of the poorly lighted bathroom and drop the key off at the front desk. The nurse tries to stop me, "I can't do this! Please don't try to stop me." On my way home I thought about how I was going to tell Mama, Robert, and Trina about my pregnancy. Would mama kill me, Robert leave me, or Trina defriend me?

As I pull up to Peyton house he looks confused. Three guys have just left from buying loose cigarettes from him. As my window goes down we align perfectly by the curb.

"Cuz, thought you were going to handle yo situation today?" Peyton knows everything.

"I was but I chickened out. It's a longs story but, I'm keeping my baby. Thank you for being there for me but here is your money back." He could not handle that I heard a voice from the sky. Peyton would look at me and laugh and tell his mom to call my mom because I was losing it. So I am keeping it simple until I can figure things out.

"You know you can ask me for anything cuz. I got you. I didn't want you to do it anyway. I kept silent because I felt like it was not my place to tell you keep the baby. I was not going to be the one who had to take care of it for eighteen years. "

"Who is dude that got you to finally open yo legs before walking down the aisle? Is he from around here?"

"No. Never!"

"Dang Cuz, we ain't all bad and dead-beat dads you know on the west side. You see me taking care of PJ all the time. Don't do me like that Ken. If a man doesn't take care of his baby it isn't cuz he is from the hood or black for that matter, it is because he is a coward and a little boy."

"Peyton that was not toward you. I have to give you your props you take care of your son but these guys around here are jerks. That's all I'm saying, my bad."

"I hope it is a boy. We need some more Lil' soldiers in the family… Well you look like you have a lot on your mind, go get you some shut eye."

"Alright, Peyton thanks again."

The last thing I am thinking about is adding soldiers to the family.

Robert has agreed to meet me later on through text and Lord knows I hope he does not turn out to be a jerk. Only time will tell. "Think baseball and tires marks" so the tears can stop rolling I tell myself in the mirror. It works every time. The flood gates are closing and now I can finally try to walk in the house past mama without being noticed. Good, she is doing a crossword puzzle. My bed feels so soft and comfortable, I think I am tripping. I'm scared mama is going to kick me out or worst, kill me.

I have an urge to use google and find out "How to tell your parents you are pregnant?" There are many suggestions but will this work on the mama that I have? Only time will tell.

Chicago XIV

The Land of Decisions

"Robert Earl, before you leave I wanted to tell you I made an appointment for Wednesday morning to look at the second location for franchising."

Shaking his head left to right Robert responds, "Ma I told you I have other plans."

Mrs. Maybeline refuses to believe that Robert has a life outside of the restaurant so she asks a rhetorical question, "What plans Robert Earl and where are you going?"

Robert turns around and closes the screen door and answers, "I am about to meet Kendra."

"Kendra, I thought you two were over." Mrs. Maybeline hits the island countertop and a clinging noise rings from her wedding band and the marble clashing.

"Well we haven't talked in two weeks but she just texted me and wants to meet."

"And you just gone go running to her like a sick puppy. Where is your pride? Make her suffer."

"Ma, I love her why would I want her to suffer?"

Mrs. Maybeline covers her heart with her hands as if she is protecting it from Robert words,

"You love her, what about me?"

"Ma I love you too, but you are my mama?" Roberts looks in the air and throws his hands out to the side.

"Look, I know what you mean Robert. Kendra does things to and for you that your mama will never do, but what woman just gets up and leave you hanging for two weeks and what type of man just forgive her so quickly?"

"I just want to hear what she has to say."

Robert grabs his mom and sits her down at the kitchen table and holds her hand.

"Ma I have something to tell you. I joined the army today."

"You did what?" Mrs. Maybeline yanks her hand away. "Over my dead body you're going to the Army. Does your father know about this? He is always trying to hurt me. He's been feeding you the Army since you were eight years old. He gives the Army all the credit for his success. I was the one who typed his papers and did study drills with him until two in the morning in order for him to receive his master's degree. Many nights I was alone after he got that degree because of business trips and start up projects and now he wants to take my boy. My baby boy."

"Ma, Pa gives you credit. I heard him say it before and I'm not your baby boy mama. I'm your son."

"Not as many times as he accolades the Army. He wanted you out this house ever since you picked me over him during the separation." Mrs. Maybeline pulls out her cell phone from her purse and begins to dial. Robert compresses her hands.

"Ma hang up the phone." Robert says while pressing the red button twice. "I've made this decision on my own. I'm a man and it's time I make my own decisions. I keep telling you I don't want to run the restaurant and you keep insisting, so I joined the army. They also have a Hockey team that I have been recruited to play on. Coach wrote a referral letter for me."

"Robert you have truly broken my heart." Mrs. Maybeline runs out of the kitchen into her bedroom. Faced with a dilemma Robert is torn between walking out the door to meet Kendra or comforting his mom. Walking out the door he ignores Mrs. Maybeline loud pleas to God and closes the door softly.

_____#_____

It is time for Robert and I to meet at the apartment. The light is on so I know he is waiting for me. Quickly the door is open and all I see is muscles, dimples, and white teeth. It has been two weeks since I smelt the scent of fried chicken, greens, lemons, onions, and Chanel men cologne.

"Hey. Come on up."

Oh no he is mad. The dimples did not even greet me. This is bad I thought to myself. Walking up the stairs I am searching for words to explain my disconnection from the relationship. The glass table in the dining room has a flower vase full of fresh sunflowers that blocks my face. I still can't believe no one lives here.

"Robert, I have something to tell you."

Abruptly Robert cuts me off and spurts, "Kendra, why have you not called me? I told you that you were going to hate me after we had sex. I should have never made love to you. Now I've lost my friend and my woman."

"Well actually you have not lost me you have made an addition to me."

Robert moves the vase to the far right to get a clearer understanding of my words, "What are you talking about? An addition to you. I don't get it."

My heart is pounding so loud I swear the little drummer boy is on my shoulders playing the score to this conversation. Before I speak let me take one last good look at him. The couch we made love on. The lips that kiss me so softly. The arms that held me close and protected me from my fears. The eyes that looked beyond my inexperience and saw a future wife in me. Because I guess now the part when the boy leaves when you get pregnant is about to happen.

"Well it is only one way to say it… I'm pregnant."

"Damn." Robert puts his head down and shakes his head from left to right. "No Kendra. Not now Kendra. Damn! Robert is standing up and pacing back and forth and holding his head.

"Damn, that was not the response I was expecting. What do you mean not now? You think I planned this?" Leaving is the best option for me because I already see where this is going.

"Not damn you're pregnant, but damn what have I done," Roberts explains while grabbing me by the waist. "Kendra I wasn't certain about what was going on between us and my mother been bugging me to run the restaurant so in defiance to her …. I signed up for the Army and I leave on the tenth of October."

"You what? How could you do that to me?" How could you make such a drastic decision without consulting the one that you claimed you love? I mean even if I have been on a sabbatical."

I love him too much to hurt him but that did not stop me from punching him softly and intensely in his chest.

"Kendra, I have been living my whole life for other people. This was not about you or to get away from you. I had to show my mom that she will no longer run my life. I had to show myself that I am my own man. Who knew you were going to get pregnant? You said you were going away to college and I just was trying to prepare myself to be the best husband and man that I could be for myself and for when you return from college. You gotta believe me!"

"I believe you." Salty tears run into my mouth and down to my shirt making a polka dot pattern.

"Babe, stop crying. I had no clue. I thought you were going away to school Ken."

"I know. You're right. You're right. I have not been communicating to you or anyone for that matter. It just everything is changing and happening so fast since I graduated from school. It feels like my life is out of control Robert."

"I am so happy that we are having a baby. Nothing has changed. I love you Kendra. I love your smile. I love your mind. I love your conversation. I love the smell of the laundry detergent you use. I love the taste of your salty tears." Robert begins to kiss me and lick one of my tears. I pull away and ask again.

"You love me?"

"Yes."

"You aren't going to turn your back on me and the baby?"

"Never. Wait…. does your mom know?"

"No."

"We can tell her together. When would you like to break the good news?"

"I would like to wait until I get bigger so she won't beat me to death and break my back."

"She won't kill you, and if she does she will have to kill me too because now you are never getting rid of me. Give me 24 hours and we can tell her together." Even though mama has not put her hands on me since I was thirteen I remember the whippings like yesterday, they were so harsh that I determine to be a perfect daughter from sixteen up until now. I know technically I am grown and out of H.S. but I am still scared of my mama.

Chicago XV

The Land of Confessions

"**R**obert Earl, is that you?" Mrs. Maybeline asked from her bedroom.

"Yes Mom."

"Why you back so early your little city slicker stood you up?" As Robert approaches her doorway he has a spiteful smile on his face. He knows the news of Kendra's pregnancy is going to send his mother to the moon but it was too important to keep it a secret, time was of the essence.

"Ma, why she has to be a city slicker? You know you should really get to know Kendra especially since she is bringing your first grandchild into the world." Robert waited five seconds for the sentence to register in Ms. Maybeline mine and five, four, three, two, one…Mrs. Maybeline sat up and pressed mute on the T.V, "Run that by me again, boy."

Robert begin to bag out of the room while stating, "You should learn to get along with the woman that is bringing your first grandchild into the world." Mrs. Maybeline gets up from her bed and begin to chase Robert down the hall.

"You are trying to kill me. You are trying to kill me. First you tell me that you joined the army and now you are telling me that you have a baby on the way by a hussy that you met less than three months ago. She saw you coming a mile away. I bet she knew about the restaurant and planned this. She is not getting any of my money. Robert am I that bad of a parent? All I ever done was love you and try to create an opportunity for you to prosper in life and this is how you reward me, by joining the Army and getting a broke tramp pregnant?"

"Mom, everything is about money with you. Yes you sent me to college but was it for my advancement or for you to have cheap labor? And how can you call my girl a broke tramp? See that's what I'm talking about you are disrespectful and controlling. A tramp is not defined by what's in a woman's wallet and you know that."

"Don't try to school me boy. Robert, you don't get it. You have just added fifty gray hairs to my hair. Leave my presence now!"

"You're in my room, leave my presence now!" Mrs. Maybeline looks around and realizes Robert is right and walks out his room.

Walking down the hall she screams, "That hussy will never get my money!"

Needing to relieve some stress Robert begins to do pushup. If only he had known Kendra was pregnant maybe he would not had made such a drastic move but it was too late and his flight to Hawaii was already booked.

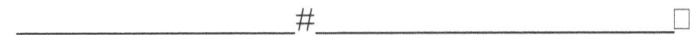

The next day Kendra texted Robert and told him that mama had a dream about fish and said that someone was pregnant. She advised him to come over so that mama could be informed of the pregnancy.

Ding Dong

"Who is it?"

"Robert ma'am."

"Hi Robert. Come on in, I'll go get Kendra."

"Ken, honey Robert is here."

Coming out of the room I make sure I have on two layers of clothes. Mama may decide to go H. A. M. on me and for the baby protection. Poor Robert I forgot to tell him to be double layered as well.

"Robert would you like some chicken?"

"No ma'am. I did not come over for dinner, we actually have something to discuss with you Mrs. Springfield." I could not believe how direct and confident he was. Maybe he thought I was playing when I said that mama don't play and she has a black belt in whipping but and taking names.

"We?" She asked while looking at Kendra and taking a seat at the table.

"Well Mama, I don't know how to say this."

"Just say it Kendra." After 60 seconds of silence and four scoots to the left away I mustered up the confidence and blurted,

"I am pregnant."

I covered my face and turned my head away to miss mama slap, but after five seconds of silence I opened my eyes to see where the slap was. Mama was in shock. She was looking into space and I could tell that a thousand thoughts were going through her mind. I kicked Robert under the table in a quest for assistance.

"Mrs. Springfield." Robert interceded.

"Don't Mrs. Springfield me, I trusted you with my daughter and now she is pregnant. Eighteen years under my care she has been baby free and a few months with you and that all has changed." Tears began to run down mama face and I joined her in crying.

"Mama I'm sorry. I'm sorry mama."

Mrs. Springfield I promise I will be there every step of the way for Kendra. I love her very much. I joined the Army to become a better man and marry her one day. I'm gonna be there for my family." Robert had the sincerest look on his face and I wanted to believe him.

A Dad's Redemption

"So let me get this straight. You got my daughter pregnant and now you are leaving for the Army. You may have fooled Kendra but I was born on a day, not yesterday. Mama gets up from the table and grabs the calendar on the wall. As she walks back to the table she hands Roberts the calendar and says, "Show me "one day" on this calendar or in the day of the week. I been looking at these things all my life and somehow my teachers, mother, and even the good Lord never taught me about this special "one day". Can you show me Robert?"

Mama was too quick for Robert. After ten seconds of silence she declared, "I think it is time for you to leave Robert." Robert stood up from the table and headed for the door.

"I am not through with you Kendra you stay put."

On the way out he tried to plead his case again but it was no use. For the rest of the night mama prayed and groaned. It was horrible hearing her cry out for the Lord to deliver me and help us but at least she did not whip the baby out of me.

Krystal, my oldest sister calls me out of the blue. She never calls me so how convenient when I tell mama I'm pregnant the phone rings. Uhm… too late to be a sister now. The damage is done already, you think? Krystal doesn't have any children. Her career as a lawyer has her biological clock on the shelf just ticking away and collecting dusk. As I see her number in the caller I. D. I cringed and hesitantly hit the green button on my cell phone to speak.

"Hello"

"Well don't sound too happy to speak to me. I know you saw my number in the caller I.D." Krystal said.

"Yeah I saw the number in the caller I. D Krystal. I have not seen it in so long I almost forgot it existed."

"Look Kendra, ain't nothing wrong with your fingers as well. I just called to say congratulations on your new addition coming to the family."

"Really did you call to congratulate me or just irritate me? Tell me how you are congratulating me on something I did not tell you anything about."

"Kendra, you know Mama can't hold water. I don't know where we went wrong but I really love you and I want to be there for you during your pregnancy."

"How?"

"You tell me what you need and I will do it."

"Well I just need to know that God forgives me and no one thinks I am a failure for having a baby without a husband for right now."

"Krystal things happen in some cases they don't happen. If you have asked God for forgiveness then He truly forgave you. Now forgive yourself. Sometimes I feel like a failure having a husband but can't conceive a child. You have to just move forward and be the best mom you can be."

"Wow, it's been so long since we had a serious conversation I kind of miss it." Instantly I look up at the ceiling to keep a tear from falling out of my eyes onto my orange pillow.

"I'm sorry that I have not been the best daughter or sister lately but I promise to do better. Congratulations again and I am so excited for you. Talk to you soon Ken. Bye."

I could hear Krystal voice crackling with tears and I wanted to scream don't go but I didn't.

Robert texted me and informed me that Mrs. Maybeline wanted to meet at the restaurant to talk. I did not know what to expect but the next day I pushed myself to meet her at noon. There is a king's spread of food on the table. The chicken is light golden brown and looks very crispy. The collard greens are not from a can impressively. The macaroni & cheese has a little burnt crust on top and baked just right. She even has some banana pudding with whip cream for dessert. This is the first time that Mrs. Maybeline and I will really sit down and talk. She is a woman of few words when it comes to me. When we finally finished lunch I was surprise that Robert was not present. He is still out on a delivery. It isn't a good day for Mrs. Maybeline because she is wearing the short black wig. The black glasses are hanging from the tip of her nose. As we dessert she looks at me with a sour look and says, "Robert tells me that you think you are pregnant."

"Well ma'am, I am pretty sure that I am pregnant." I said with a look on my face like …really!

"He also told me that it may be his."

"Well ma'am that is incorrect".

Mrs. Maybeline begins to smile and then I say, "It is absolutely his."

She clinches the golden cloth napkin and takes a drink of water.

"Well I know many people in many places, were you going to keep it?"

"Yes ma'am."

"Are you sure?"

"Yes ma'am."

"Good, if you need anything let me know."

I could tell by her tone that the "let me know" was not genuine.

"Well help yourself to the food I need to cut this meeting short. I have been scheduled for an extemporaneous conference call in fifteen minutes and I need to prep."

As I sit there at the table I text Robert and inform him that the meeting is over. So far so good both of our parents knew about the pregnancy and we both were still alive. There was only one person left to tell, Trina. While driving home from Maybeline's Greens & Things for the Soul I text Trina and ask her when we can talk. She advises me that she will be able to do a video conference in two hours. On my way home I call mama to see if she needs anything while I'm out and she replies,, "I'm fine just hurry home before it gets too dark." Mama has already begun to be over protective of me. I ain't even three months pregnant yet. She calls me whenever I am out pass 8 p.m. and actually seem happy that her first grandchild is coming into the world. She even threw away all of the hot sauce in the kitchen cabinets. She permed my hair and told me I would not be getting another until I had the baby. She says she is teaching me the ins and outs of a healthy pregnancy. After all, I did fulfill my promise of graduating out of High School without a child.

Tears begin to roll down my face as I think about the next eight months of my pregnancy and going through it alone without my friend and man. I wipe my tears and dial Trina's number as I walk to my room. Her face pops on the screen. I position the phone on my orange pillow so I can have my hands free.

"Hey girl, what's up Ken?"

"Nothing much, wait a second girl." I walk to the closet to take my hoodie off and return to the bed.

"Dang Ken, somebody is gaining a few pounds. Your booty trying to get big." Under any other circumstances that would have been a compliment. This thickness that Trina was noticing was migrating to my breast and hips. I mean who doesn't want a little junk in the trunk or be "thicker than a snicker" but I knew this was only the beginning. My skin also was beginning to become very clear and soft.

"I would say thank you but not this time. Trina I have something to tell you but first I need to know if you love me?"

"Kendra, you are scaring me. Is everything ok?"

"Trina, do you love me?" I need to hear yes before I could go on.

"Yes Kendra I love you. Now what is going on?"

"Well….."

"I found out that I am pregnant." Trina begins to holler "OMG!!! "

I begin to cry and put my head into my hands. Trina began to hyperventilate and walk in circles in her dorm room.

"Ken, how could you let this happen? I mean did you all use protection? Tell me you used protection." She was the first person to ask me that question. "It was not planned; I got caught up in the moment. I thought since he had been with other girls he knew what to do."

"Ken, does Mama know?"

"Yes."

"Does Robert know?"

"Yes, but he has signed up for the army."

"Hell naw, this buster gets my friend pregnant and is leaving. Kendra what are you going to do?"

"He is not like that Trina. He loves me and he joined the Army to become a better man. I am going to keep my baby and have it and all by myself if I have to."

"Ken, I feel like if I was here this would not have happened. I wasn't here to protect you this summer. I am sorry Kendra. I'm sorry. We will get through this together." This was the second time that phrase was said to me by two people who were literally leaving me in Chicago while they travel the world.

"Trina I begged Robert to make love to me. I am not so innocent. I wanted him and he wanted me. I just didn't think on my first round my sins would catchup with me." Trina promised to send me articles on pregnancy and fashion. She assured me that she would come home for winter break and the following summer of 2011 and spend it with me and the new addition. Uncertain of the sex of my baby we just called it the new addition to the glam squad. If it was a girl she would be a Diva. If it was a boy he would be a Don.

Chicago XVI

The Land of Goodbyes

R obert is coming over to say goodbye today and I am devastated. October 10, 2010 came too quick. The plan is for him to return a better man but the process is unbearable and besides he is perfect to me already. He recognizes every time I wear a new dress or accessory. Last week at the doctor's office he noticed that I cut my hair one inch shorter. Sometimes I think he notices too much, like the time he noticed that I did not have my regular caramel frappe. I ordered a sweet tea and he immediately asked, "What's wrong Kendra, no frappe?" The doctor gave me a labor date of May 23. I am having a Summer baby. Trina and I use to always say if we ever got pregnant we hope it was through the winter because maternity daisy dukes are not cool. Well at least I will be able to still have July and August to show the world the blessing that God has given Robert and I. We heard the heart beat and it sounded better than James Brown "The Big Payback". I could record my baby's fast heartbeat and listen to it driving around,

Ding Dong

"Mama can you get the door? It's Robert."

"OK sweetie." As she goes to open the door I already have my Kleenex under the sheet with me. This pregnancy has turned me into the biggest cry baby. Damn this man is fine. Every time I see him I fall in love all over again. While hugging him I try to say hey sweetie but a whisper of "Don't go" comes out instead.

"Ken I have to go I gave my word and signed a contract with the government. It's just training for ten weeks. I will be back before you can say "bobble baby bumps burst blueberry biscuits."

"What?" Only Robert would have a tongue twister in the middle of a dilemma like this. It's one of the things I love about him, his humor and random outburst keeps me on my toes.

I will be back before you can say "bobble baby bumps burst blueberry biscuits."

"Oh yeah?"

"Yeah."

"Bobble bumps blueberry biscuits burst baby. Dang it I said it wrong! It is a stupid saying anyway." Shaking my head I grab him closer. "Promise me that you will return to me."

"I promise you Kendra Latrice Springfield that I will return to you and only you sweetie. Now take care of my baby and I will be home for Christmas."

I could tell Robert was leaving so he would not get mushy. So I spared his manhood and let him leave. Turning over in my bed I suffocate myself in my pillow and begin to cry and whale. I have never loved anyone like this before. The longest we have been apart is the two weeks I stop talking to him. Now I have to go ten weeks without, being protected by his strong arms and seeing his dimples. Luckily his cologne is on my robe and it will not be getting washed anytime soon. After an hour Mama finally stuck her head inside the door to check on me.

"How are you holding up?"

"Barely Mama. I know you are not too fond of him but I really love Robert. He is really a nice guy."

"Well Ken, I don't hate the boy for the record. I just wish circumstances were a little different. I know you are sad that he is leaving but at least he is not going to jail for ten weeks. Maybe he will return a better man for you and the baby like he plans. Lord knows I pray he does."

"He will mama."

"I see it in his eyes. He loves me."

"Well Ken only time will tell…. only time will tell. I'm going to the supermarket do you need anything?"

"Yeah, I would like some salt n sour potato chips and a dill pickle. Oh and don't forget the strawberry ice cream."

Mama had warned me earlier on about the crazy cravings and mood swings. That night I went to bed with my robe and orange pillow to comfort me for the night.

_____#_____

Today is my birthday, December 22, 2010. Trina flight kept getting canceled due to the snow storm so she has decided to stay in sunny California for the winter break.   I am on Christmas break as well.   Harper College turned out to be a great decision.   The professors are way cooler and curse while teaching, imagine that. They also let you curse when responding to their lessons.   I must admit it took me awhile to get use to that. Finding a maternity outfit is really awkward. Everything is so blah. It's bad enough you have a bulging stomach why can't the fashion industry make prettier maternity clothes?   Glitter and swag seem to be off limits in the maternity fashion world.   Robert and I have a date tonight and we are going to go to Christmas party for Maybeline's Green & Things for the Soul employees.   Luckily, Macy's had their holiday sale and I was able to find a red dress that was sexy and festive.

Mama is in the kitchen making caramel cakes for her customary church members who have put in a special order for their holiday feasts. The smell of cake batter is making me nausea. Growing up that sweet smell of eggs, flower, sugar, butter, corn powder, and salt represented two things, holidays and family. I call on her to help me zip the back of my dress.

"Mama…..Ma"

"Yes Kendra is everything ok?" Mama said while rushing into my room with flower on her hands.

"Everything is fine. I needed help with my dress zipper but your hands are dirty."

"Soap and water can take care of that I'll be right back."

Mama goes in the kitchen and I grab my phone and text Robert to let him know I am running a little behind.

"They're all clean. Turn around so I can zip your dress. Oh Kendra this is a beautiful dress. I want you to enjoy your birthday tonight and don't let that crazy lady Maybeline raise your blood pressure."

"I'll try not to. Pray that the good Lord give me a double portion of patience tonight."

"I hear a horn blowing. It's Robert. You look beautiful, be careful, and don't dance too hard.

Robert eyes light up and his dimples greet me when I open the door.

"Lady in red. You look stunning Kendra."

Walking to the car was almost impossible for the ice that was on the ground. Thirsty Ted had shoveled earlier and put salt down. I guess those quarters pay off in the long run. Robert slowly walks me to the passenger side of the car.

"Stunning? That's a first." I reply as I gently sit in my seat and reach for my seat belt. As Robert walks around the car I can smell his cologne. It is a new fragrance.

"So I see you have a new fragrance on."

"How you know?"

"I notice everything about you?"

"Yeah right?"

"I do. I notice that you have a fresh haircut. I notice that your muscles in your arms are bigger. I notice that you are the love of my life." Robert blushes and continues to drive towards the party. He is playing the Isley Brothers Let me know. He reaches for my hand and holds it as he drives. As we pull in the parking lot he finds a park and reaches for a bag in the back of the car.

"I know I said it earlier but happy birthday again Kendra. I love you and I notice everything about you as well."

"Oh yeah?"

"Yeah."

"Like what?"

"I notice that you got your hair done today and it has grown about two inches. I notice that you got your eyebrows done. I notice that your lips are my weakness. I notice that you think your legs are your greatest asset but it is your eyes. I notice that every time I see you I fall deeper and deeper in love with you."

"Aw bae." As I rub the back of Roberts head and kiss him he directs me to my bag.

"Here is your birthday gift. Open your bag."

"OK, OK." Robert is more excited than me. I open the bag and see a pastel green box and an envelope. I grab the envelope first and open the card. It has a $100 visa card. I open the box next and it has a Tiffany necklace with a key pendant. The card reads,

"You hold the key to my heart. Love Robert."

"Bae this is the sweetest thing anyone has ever done for me."

"You deserve it. You are probably the first woman to ever open a card first before a tiffany bag. Now let's get inside before my mom begins to blow my phone up with calls."

Robert puts the necklace on my neck before we enter the party. It was the perfect accessory for my dress. All night we stepped the night away. He is introducing me to all of his mom's colleagues as his fiancé way different than Mrs. Maybeline description a friend. After a while my feet begin to hurt so I sat at our table and watched Robert and other people make a fool of themselves on the dance floor. One guy was doing the snake. That dance was played out ten years ago but you could not tell him anything. He was determined to keep it in style. Mrs. Maybeline finally came to the table.

"Hi Kendra. I hear today is your birthday."

"Yes it is."

"How old are you?"

"I made nineteen today."

"Oh I remember that age I was in my prime at college and playing tennis like Venus and Serena. Oh well, in your situation with the baby on the way tennis or any other sport is out of the question. Happy birthday and remember if you ever need anything you let me know. It's still not too late…"

"I'm fine. Thank you."

Mrs. Maybeline walks away with a smile on her face. I can't believe she wished me a happy birthday and gave me an invitation to kill her grandchild at the same time. I hope none of her DNA is in my baby. That conversation was a buzz kill and I don't even drink. As I locate Robert I inform him I am ready to leave. While driving home I can't help but to ask,

"Do you want the baby?"

"What?"

"Do you want to have this baby?"

"Of course I want my baby. Why would you ask me that? Kendra I will bring you strawberry ice cream in the middle of the night? I won't miss any doctor appointments? Just don't terminate my child. So why would you ask me that?"

"Just forget it." I was afraid to tell him how cruel Mrs. Maybeline was. If he had to choose between me and her I am sure she would win. After all she is his mother.

"Kendra promise me you won't ask me that again. I am getting ready for my 2nd deployment in thirty days and I need to know that you know how much I love you and my child. I am doing this for us baby. I love you."

"OK. I believe you."

Arriving in front of my house I just want to go inside and be under my mother. I kiss Robert good night and slowly get escorted inside.

Chicago XVII

The Land of Movement

The gender of my baby is a girl. Robert and I have decided to name her Kimberly Rose Thompson. I miss him dearly and can't wait to see him again. He is deployed until May. We brought 2011 in the apartment above the restaurant. Robert had red wine while I perpetrated and had cranberry juice. The glasses we drank from was crystal and when we toasted it sounded like a cling from Heaven. It echoed and sent ripples of joy, romance, and love through the front room. He has promised to be here for the delivery. Mrs. Maybeline gave me a surprise baby shower but it was just a show she put on. She did not have anyone there that I knew, not even Mama. In fact no one brought me presents they just wanted to see the girl that "claimed" to be pregnant by Robert. We are talking about a family that has an apartment just for the frozen chicken and fresh fruit to reside in so I know they got money. The crowd of spectators were beginning to make me feel real irritated so I faked nausea just to leave.

"Kendra why are you slamming doors around here is everything okay."

Should I say yes and just ignore the fact that I was humiliated or should I be honest and fall into her arms because right now I need a hug.

"Mama you want the truth?"

"Of course, what's wrong Ken." Mama takes off her apron and walk into my rook my eyes begin to water up. She sits on the bed next to me and it just feels so good to have someone around that is genuine.

"I had a baby shower today?

"How did you do that and I was not invited?"

"Mrs. Maybeline call herself giving me a surprise baby shower."

"Oh really, well where are the presents?"

"Exactly Mama, no one brought me or Kimberly anything. They just whispered, laughed, and pointed until I could not take it anymore and I played sick just to get out of there. It was only food as if I can't afford to buy my own food."

"Kendra hand me your phone. Mrs. Maybeline gone make me have to go to the altar."

"Ma don't call her."

"How dare you give my daughter a baby shower and … don't invite me and… don't bring any presents."

"Ma please don't call her. She is never gonna change."

"Only because you asked me Kendra. This time, I will not call. I don't want to stress you and my granddaughter out, but when I see her it is not going to be nice."

Robert writes me every week and sends me money every month. He is the perfect husband to be. Mama has forgiven him and decided to make an appointment with Dr. Cebalis for the second opinion. The diagnosis is glaucoma but they are going to perform an operation that will add another twenty years of vision to her eyes.

Pastor Jenkins called us to the office this Sunday and informed us that the church would be praying for us and not to worry. He assured us no one was going to expunge us. Mama was worried about the missionary board at church expunging her off the board. Her daughter was having a baby out of wedlock and the father not present. To some I was a disgrace and to others I was the hot topic of the month. Once my belly got big and Pastor Jenkins did not remove me from the sanctuary. Three more young adults got pregnant who were not married. The church mothers were concerned and started a virtuous woman group. They teach us lessons on cooking, sewing, cleaning, praying, fasting, and forgiving. They said we were going to be doing a lot of all the above as parents.

Kimberly has not greeted me today with flips and jumps inside my belly and I am worried. Holding my orange pillow on my bed I can't help but begin to cry. She will never meet Pa. She will never know how his mustache pokes your cheek like a porcupine when he hugs and kisses you. She will never smell his Da Brut cologne when he is leaving for work. She will never witness him singing to the temptations on Christmas Eve. I can only begin to plea to God and her not to leave me like Pa and to please kick inside my belly.

PLEASE DON'T GO

Please don't go, continue to grow.

I promise to be the best mom I know.

I want to play with your ten little toes.

I will love you as long as times goes.

A Dad's Redemption

Months have passed and it's now getting close to my delivery. Robert is due back home May 20th. On my way to the restroom a gush of water trickles down my legs.

"Mama I am so sorry. I thought I could hold it. The Judge Mathis show was so good, I was trying to wait for a commercial."

"That is not pee Kendra running down your legs. That is your water breaking. You my dear are about to become a mom."

"Wait! Robert is not here. Call him now Mama and see if he can get an emergency leave."

"I'll call him Ken, but it's up to Kimberly if she wants to wait for her daddy."

Robert has gotten the clearance to arrive in Illinois for Kimberly's birth. I do not know what to expect in labor. A hundred thoughts are going through my head. The psychology class has educated me on how to nurture Kimberly with hugs instead of hundreds of dollars. I am on maternity leave from the second-hand store until August. It's May 3, 2011 at 2 p.m. in the afternoon and I am on my way in an ambulance to have our baby.

Labor lasted 24 hours and at 8 p.m. the next evening I was holding Kimberly Rose Thompson in my arms. She weighed five pounds and six ounces. Her hair is black and curly. God blessed her with her daddy's dimples. Robert fainted from all the blood, screaming, and seeing the crowning of her head. The nurse went to retrieve him from the recovery room. As he walks in the room I can

tell he is a little embarrassed. His head hangs low and he would not look me in the eyes.

"Ken, I am so sorry for fainting. I have never seen anything like that in my life." As Robert comes closer I see his facial expression change when laying eyes on Kimberly, "She so…

"Beautiful I know!

"I was gonna say dark." Robert murmured disapprovingly.

"And what's wrong with that?" I was confused because his dark complexion was the very thing that attracted me to him.

"Kendra, everyone doesn't love dark skin the way that you do. Some people see black and they see bad, think bad, and they do bad things to you."

"What are you talking about Robert? Some of the best things in life are dark or black."

"Like what Ken?"

"Dark Chocolate"

"What else?" Robert inquired.

"Black Friday."

"What else?"

"The darker the berry the sweeter the juice." I said laughing.

"I'm serious. Why did God give her my complexion?"

"Look Robert, I love you and especially your dark complexion. God gave her more than your skin tone. He gave her your dimples and I am sure she has your sweet spirit. In fact if you were lighter I would not have even looked your way. Your skin color is dominant and I am honored that God blessed her with her daddy's complexion. Now give your beautiful baby a kiss. She does not need to be welcomed in the world to negativity and shame."

The next couple of days Robert came over to the house to see Kimberly every night at seven o'clock. He was very concerned about how drastically the neighborhood had changed. There were no more familiar faces on the block. Robert wanted to spend the night with Kimberly and I but Mama did not allow it since we were not married. It aches his heart to leave us at night. On this particular night I asked Mama to watch Kimberly as I walked Robert to the car. As we are walking to the corner we hear this voice come from behind us.

"Well well well it is my lucky day. It is time for me to get my ass whip." Oh my God Lil' Mike! Robert looks confuse and says, "Sorry Bruh you have the wrong people." I try to act as if I don't know Lil' Mike and pray he goes away, but he blows my cover. "Kendra is this the guy who is going to whip my ass? Is this your boyfriend?"

Lil' Mike had a tone that was too confident. How could he remember a conversation from almost a year ago? Did Lil' Mike seriously have nothing to do in life but wait for my boyfriend to come on the block? Frustrated, Robert turns around and put me in back of him and says, "I told you wrong people. Now if an ass whipping is what you looking for I can help you out with that."

I had never seen this side of Robert before. He turned into this confident, strong, and skillful trained body guard. He turned into the king of the jungle and his eyes went from hazel brown to killer brown. I tried to come in between Lil' Mike and Robert but he became so strong and before I knew it he had Lil' Mike in head lock. "Say bruh I don't want no trouble I just came over her to see my lady and my baby girl do we have a problem?" Lil' Mike replied "no" to my surprise and Robert released him. He told Robert and I quote. "You'll see me again dude sooner than later." Lil' Mike ran through the alley and Robert yelled at me to go in the house and lock the door. He said he would call me and I knew then I had a lot of explaining to do.

After explaining all of Lil' Mike failed attempts to hit on me Robert understood the confrontation. I did not know Robert had a temper to him. He did tell me he was a black belt but dang. That was like a scene from a Steven Segal movie.

The phone is ringing and I am scared to answer it. I don't know what Robert is going to say. Here goes nothing…

"Ken, I passed five crack heads from the car to me getting to the front door. Why are there so many teddy bears and empty bottles on all of the corners? I can't have you and my baby living under these conditions. You guys are coming to live in the apartment. I am not accepting no for an answer."

"Robert, what about Mama? I just can't leave her alone like this."

"She can come too. There are three bedrooms in the spare apartment. My child should not and will not grow up in this type of environment. The school district is great in Elmhurst and the crime rate is significantly lower."

"Well, I will think about it and talk to Mama."

I knew Mama was not leaving her home. That was the house that her and Pa had decorated together. Our house was their love nest. I offered to show her the apartment above the restaurant but expectedly she declined.

Chicago XVIII

The Land of Initiation

inally Mrs. Maybeline called and invited me over to the house after Kimberly made one month old. She attributed her schedule at the restaurant for not seeing Kimberly sooner.

As I walk in the door, Mrs. Maybeline grabs Kimberly out of my arms and take her into the other room. Where the family was patiently waiting. She looked surprised at her complexion the same way Robert did. I was beginning to see that look often at the doctor's office, grocery store, and at church. All of Robert's family was there and crowded Kimberly and took her to Big Ma. I had never met Big Ma so I followed. As I walked in the room Big Ma was beautiful. She was a frail lady of not more than 120 pounds with big cream-colored pearls and hot-pressed gray curls. She has on a beautiful mint green dress that makes her complexion glow goldenly. She opens her arms to receive Kimberly. Then surprisingly, Big Ma begins taking my baby's socks off. I ask Robert what she was doing and he replied, "Big Ma can tell our family members by our feet and hands. Every Thompson has gone through this ritual." Big Ma rubs Kimberly's feet and plays with her hands and then looks at Mrs. Maybeline and smiles. The whole family burst into the room with pink clothes, furniture, pampers, and milk. I've never seen Robert look so happy. I guess my baby passed the traditional DNA test.

We need another Big Lou party in the neighborhood. Lil' Mike and Nino are really into it bad. Lil' Mike died this week in a drive by while standing on the corning saying his famous line, "Loose squares two for a dollar, loose squares." Trina and I opted out of the funeral due to a heads up we got that retaliation was going to be attempted by his crew. Sadly, at Lil' Mike funeral two more people got shot. Even though Robert and Lil' Mike got into it he was still a part of our neighborhood and I felt sad that he died.

It's August already I have decided to move in the apartment above the restaurant. It is already furnished and that is a catch 22 for me. I dreamed of furnishing my own apartment. I have five seasons of watching HGTV under my belt and I am qualified and certified to pick my own color scheme and kitchen backdrop. I will admit Mrs. Maybeline style was very modern and chic but it felt like her apartment since I did not decorate it. It was my second-year anniversary at the second-hand store but the hours are being cut due to the lack of donations coming in and the customer purchases. Being in that apartment brought back so many memories. This is where my life took a detour for the better or worse is yet to be determined.

"Hello Kendra, welcome." I would say thank you to Mrs. Maybeline but she did not knock.

"I took the liberty to add a second refrigerator so that the restaurant stock would not be combined with your hot wings and French fries."

"Um I don't have hot wings and French fries in my freezer." She ignores me and continues.

"Robert informed me that he will be paying three hundred dollars of the six hundred I am charging for rent. The next nine months with him gone away to train to become an aviation officer will be bitter sweet but we will manage, us Thompson women always do. Is this feasible for you?"

"Yes ma'am."

"Good we should get along just fine then. I'm just a flight of stairs away call me if you need me, but I'm sure you will be fine." Mrs. Maybeline walked out the door.

She did not even acknowledge Kimberly in the front room playing. She is so mean! She has this sarcastic way to offer help and let you know not to take her up on it. Mrs. Maybeline makes me want to call my Mama and say I love you but I have not talked to Trina lately so I will call ma in a sec.

Ring ring

"Hello"

"Hey Trina!"

"Hey Ken, how is everything going in the Windy City?"

"I can't complain. I'm still working and going to school part time. Kimberly is getting so big."

"How are you doing?"

"Girl I thought I knew fashion until I got to California. People are at the grocery store in Versace Ken. My classmates come to school like they are going to the Grammy's. Can you believe I had to step my game up?"

"No way!"

"Yes way. So how does it feel having your own place now?"

"It feels weird. I wait for mama to come home sometimes and then I realize we don't stay together anymore. But she calls all the time and babysits Kimberly for me which helps out a lot because babysitting is so expensive."

"Yeah I know what you mean. My sister and Jessica miss me but primarily my sister. Daycare is whipping her butt. It's weird being down here without any familiar faces. At first I was scared but I have met some really nice people."

"I hope not too nice I don't want no valley girl taking my friend away."

"Never. I love you Ken…. however I have been bad already."

"What you do Trina? Tell me how much you went over on your visa Platinum."

"Worst Ken."

"Worst?"

"I think my professor Mr. Cunningham likes me. Well I know he likes me because we kissed."

"OHHH MYY GODDDD!!"

"Ken he is 27 years old, Caucasian, and has a body that was made for the front cover of sports magazine."

"He's White Trina?"

"White."

"How does white saliva taste?"

"He smokes so it has a hint of nicotine and peppermint. He's a bad ass too. He rides a Harley motorcycle."

"But we never discussed inter racial relationships Trina, you have changed the game"

"I never seen a man other than a black man that made me blush. I wore my Chanel perfume and he knew the name of the fragrance."

"That's epic Trina. He is into fashion too?"

"He told me he could lose his job if anyone finds out but I am worth it. I don't know anyone here to tell and why would I. He is perfect."

"Well if you are happy I am happy for you. Just be careful and follow your own advice. Be a lady at all times and it's not what a man says it's what he shows you. Does he offer you the last of the popcorn on a date? Does he open doors? Does he text while at the dinner table? Does he have his phone on top security? Remember that Diva! You were always the crazy and courageous one, I'm not surprised at all. Just when I thought we were even you switch races on me."

Well, I really called to get your new address because I made the cutest dress for Kimberly. It was a class project and I got an A on it."

"Oh Ken, you are spoiling her already. Send it to Mama address. Mrs. Maybeline be tripping real hard. She's like the sergeant around here."

"Ken, she still tripping? Did she not get the memo that her son is not her husband? I'm going to send it to her."

"Trina stop playing don't do that."

"Dear Mrs. Maybeline…"

"Trina! OK OK I will send the dress to your Ma's talk to you soon."

It was nice hearing from Trina. The winter was coming soon so Robert wrote me and his mom and told her to give me his car. Like Mama says, "God may not come when you want Him but He is always right on time." Mrs. Maybeline gave me the keys to the white Toyota Corolla and told me I had to keep up the insurance payments.

I agreed. Luckily the car was paid for so that was the only expense associated with the vehicle. For the next year Robert and I communicated through email and letters. Occasionally he would call but the training was really intense for him. He was training to be a pilot and he often shared that he had to study twice as hard in order to stay in the top ranking of his class. Kimberly was learning to say da da from his pictures around the house. Her first steps were such a big deal but I begin to cry because Robert was not there to share it with us. It was so unexpected she pulled up on the couch and walked to her favorite toy doll Molly on the other side of the room. As I looked out the window from the plant room I notice the sun was not shining and the sky was grey. On a day many would think was a gloomy day I though the sky looked like gray cotton candy. I was inspired to write.

My Favorite Color

Gray gets along with everything.

It's not bossy like the color red,

Or too loud like fire sirens that mute conversations while passing by.

Some people think gray is boring,

Like the stories my uncle Rickie tells,

Or Thanksgiving Day without a turkey.

Gray isn't too soft like ice cream neglected on a Summer day.

Gray is the perfect mixture of black and white,

It is the color of peace.

Barack Obama is our first gray President.

Gray complements its surroundings,

Like an earring to an ear.

Enhancing beauty,

Like a pearl necklace to a neck.

Gray is safe like a child in a mother's arm.

My Daughter

You are the love of my life.

I love you so much without a doubt.

I will always be there to help you out, through the good and also the bad.

You are the first fruits of my seed.

I will give you the resources to succeed

Your strength and health are what I pray.

I will love and cherish you every day.

I know sometimes I will seem a little tough, but that's just to prepare you for this world-*baby its rough.*

See you are going to experience some things you won't understand, but trust in the LORD it is in his perfect plan.

I tell you I love you every day, so when that nappy head boy comes alone and say it, your sunshine you won't give away.

Know that you are beautiful and you are loved.

If I should ever leave you, remember you have GOD up above.

HE will guide you through this series called life.

Always strive to be more than just a wife.

Strive to be the best.

Remember it might be a test.

The world is here for you to take.

So do something big and history aim to make.

Kimberly begins to cry for attention as I pick her up from playing with her toy blocks she says, "ma-ma, ma-ma MA MA!" At that moment I was so over taken by emotions. "That's right ma-ma." I grabbed my phone and begin to record her. I wanted to save moments like these for when Robert returns. As I prepare Kimberly diaper bags to visit mama my phone rings. It's my job, I wonder who called off today they must want me to come in.

"Hello"

"Hi Kendra, this is Cedrick." Cedrick is my manager at the second-hand store. He's a very friendly and flamboyant fella. I never saw him with dirty nails or pants without suspenders.

"Hi Ced, do you need me to come in early today?"

"Well Kendra, as I am looking over the payroll we keep going over payroll hours. So I need to lay you off until business picks back up."

"What! Why me. Don't my seniority and customer reviews count for something?"

"It does, but your availability is what is crippling you due to your school schedule."

"Well thanks for calling me and saving me the embarrassment."

"Kendra I promise to call you when business picks up. You are one of our finest employees. This really was a hard decision to make."

Crap! What am I going to do now? The mailman is dropping packages through the door down stairs. Let me try to beat Mrs. Maybeline to the mailbox. Great, just what I need, a letter from Robert with bird drawings on the envelope. Robert is psychic. A check for five hundred dollars falls from the letter and it reads:

Dear Kendra & Kimberly,

How are my two special ladies doing? Fine I hope. I am writing to say that I will be home soon. Thank you for the pictures and the bags full of goodies. The Sour Patch Kids candy made me famous with the crew. Your pictures get me through the long hours of routine pilot simulations and long studying hours. I do it for you two. I endure so that I can take care of my soon to be wife and family. Kendra enclosed is a check for you to purchase something nice for the two of you and to help out with the insurance on the car. I love you Kendra and I count down the days to seeing your smile again. As soon as I get home I want to get married. Start planning Kendra, I can't go another day without you being my wife.

Robert XOXO

Instantly I bow down on the hallway stairs and begin to thank and praise God.

"Lord you are my provider and I thank you for allowing me to experience your goodness."

This letter gives me hope that Kimberly and I will be OK and that God is truly looking out for us. Instantly I call Trina,

Ring, ring

"Hello"

"Trina! Girl guess what?"

"What?"

"Robert told me to start planning the wedding and I want you to make my wedding dress."

"OMG! Kendra you want me to make your dress? I am so honored. Thank you for believing in me."

"Trina, I have never planned a wedding before."

"Well, duh, you think I would know that since we are only 20 and have been together through thick and thin."

"I know right, but I'm glad we are going to go through this together."

"Ken, I am so happy for you. Maybe I misjudged Robert after all."

"All I wanted people to see was that Robert is a good guy and he really loves me Trina, He really loves me."

"Well, Ken look in some magazines for styles that you like and let me know what you come up with. Wait, does your mama know about this?"

"No, I just read the letter five minutes ago."

Well, call her and talk it over with her and then call me back."

"OK, pick up the phone when I call."

"Don't I always…bye."

Trina was right. I needed my mama input on this but over the phone was not the best way to tell her to start picking out her mother of the bride dress.

The next day I went on my school job board and applied for some student positions available. I did not have it in me to let Robert or Mrs. Maybeline know I was unemployed. Besides, my unemployment would not be for long. Pastor Jenkins teaches that a wife is a help meet not a liability. Mrs. Maybeline already seemed a little agitated by Roberts love and kindness to me. If she found out he was the only bread winner in the relationship it would validate her views of me. You would have thought by now she would have accepted us but she was stubborn as a bull. It was time to meet with Mama and tell her that Robert had given me the green light to start planning the wedding. I was going to leave it up to him to break the news to Mrs. Maybeline. That was a battle I was not willing to fight, not alone anyway. Mama and I are meeting at IHOP for breakfast on this Saturday morning. Mrs. Maybeline had the morning off and took Kimberly to the grocery store with her to enjoy samples in the aisles. Sitting down at the table sweat is blistering on my forehead. I decided to jump right into as soon as the waiter brings Mama her coffee.

"Ma"

"Yes baby."

"Robert wrote me earlier this week and wants me to begin planning the wedding."

"Oh that's great honey. What did he say exactly?"

"Well he said that he can't take another day without me being his wife and to start planning the wedding. He should be home in two months."

"Wow it's been 11 months already?'

"Yeah, and I am counting the days. Are you ready to pick out your mother of the bride dress mama?"

"I guess if I'm not I better get ready. Your dad and I went to the courthouse. Never planned a wedding. Krystal been planning her wedding since sixteen years of age so there was little we had to do beside cut the check. I have attended many and I am sure we can get through this. What color scheme would you like for your wedding?"

"I think mint green and cream would be a good color."

"That's a nice combination. What about pink and cream?"

"I've never been a pink girl Mama you know that."

"Wait a minute. Who is paying for the wedding? I mean we do have a nice savings that Pa left for us but have you discussed this with Robert?"

"Not yet. Well I would start thinking about your color scheme and your dress style and the rest should be easy when we determine a budget."

"OK Mama. Thank you for not being mad."

"Kendra I am not mad at you or Robert I just want you to make sure you know what you are doing. At your age everything seems peaches and cream until reality hit and life teaches you a lesson. But the truth is me and your dad met at a young age and fell in love and truly was together until death did us part. My prayer is that this is true love for you. I love you and only want the best for you."

Mama and I enjoyed our breakfast and it was a good day and now I am officially planning a wedding.

Three weeks passed and no one has called me for an interview. I had to do something I did not want to do. I called Krystal and told her about my unemployment. Within hours she had money gram me one thousand dollars. She said it was her pleasure to help out and asked me to take some professional pics of Kimberly and send them to her. Wow, God gave me my sister back. Krystal promised not to tell Mama. She also informed me that she still had connections in the down town area of Chicago and she would make a few a call on my behalf.

It's been weeks since I communicated with Robert. It is longer than our usual four-day gap of communication. I guess I will write him a letter in my favorite window.

A Dad's Redemption

Dear Robert,

I hope all is well. You are truly adored, loved, and missed on a daily basis. Kimberly is walking like she is training for a marathon. The apartment and the car are such a blessing and I thank you for loving us the way that you do. You are such an incredible man and I feel like the luckiest woman alive. I can't wait to kiss you and put my fingers inside your dimples. Stay strong. You are as smart as the other guys and remember you can do all things through Jesus Christ which strengthens you. Here is a picture of what's waiting for you when you get home.

Love,

Kendra

A picture of Kimberly and I was included in the letter. We truly miss him and it is time for his return home but, I understand and respect his passion for leadership, growth, family, and freedom.

My fingers are feeling like magnets to this pen. Another poem is coming to the surface:

If I Never Knew You

If I never knew you how boring life would be,

no one to care for, no one to set me free.

You take me to a place where only smiles and laughs survive.

You take me to a place that makes me happy I'm alive.

This place has no name, no physical address.

It does exist and with you I can express (my feeling, my concerns, and my dreams).

If I never knew you, who would I tell my secrets to?

Who would give me a shoulder to lean on and for my tears tissue?

If I never knew you, who would help me pay my bills?

Who would understand and not judge and help me provide meals?

If I never knew you who would understand,

that I get tired, I'm not perfect, and I am just a woman?

If I never knew you, who would I love,

who would hold me, kiss me, and fit me like a glove?

Thank God I know you.

Thank God you care.

Thank God we love each other

Thank God we will always be a pair.

Krystal connections came through and I have an interview coming up at the County Clerk Office. Another week had gone by and no response from Robert. I'm concerned for him. Lord knows how hard the drills must have been.

"Kimberly let's go see nana and get some pudding."

"Nana" Kimberly responds and runs to the door.

"Well hello strangers." Mrs. Maybeline says as we walk in the door.

"Hi Mrs. Maybeline."

I still called her Mrs. Maybeline because she has not given me the green light or the feeling to call her mom. Finally, Mrs. Maybeline faces lights up when she sees Kimberly. My visit to the restaurant is also infrequent because I like my mama's cooking and although Mrs. Maybeline can cook it is more of a loyal thang.

"What's going on Kendra and how is my baby girl doing all pretty in pink."

"She is doing well. She is getting big and missing her dad. Have you heard from Robert lately?"

"You know Ken I was going to ask you the same thing. Last I heard he was doing some intensive drills and he promised to call me with good news. Don't worry he is fine he is just kicking butt and taking names."

"Yeah you are right. Is it alright if Kimie gets some banana pudding?"

"Sure my grandbaby can get whatever she wants." As Mrs. Maybeline hands me the cup of banana pudding I couldn't help but notice that she has hired a new cashier and a cute one at that. She began to speak about us like she knew us or had been briefed on us.

"Is this the baby? Oh my goodness she is so pretty and chocolate like her daddy."

As I extend my hand to get more info on this chick that just described my man and my baby as chocolate Mrs. Maybeline interjects and says,

"Kendra this is Leslie the new cashier. She and Robert went to H.S. together and she also attended Spellman in Atlanta. She's back home now and I agreed to let her help out a little with the restaurant. Robert left some big shoes to be filled."

"Hi Lisa."

"Leslie"

"Oh I'm sorry Leslie nice to meet."

"Like wise."

Why do women get girls name wrong on purpose? It is like the most subtle way to say you are not even important enough for me to remember your name but it has to come across as an honest mistake. I laughed going all the way up the stairs. I remembered her name and

I also recognized her game. She came back for my man and the next time she associates him with chocolate in front of me it's going to be a problem.

Chicago XIX

The Land of Heartbreak

Robert had not responded to any of my letters and another two weeks had passed. No congratulations on the new job. No feedback on me and Krystal new found relationship. No insurance payment. No inquiries on the progress of the wedding planning. This was so unlike him. I decided to google how to contact his Superior. Mrs. Maybeline would never give me the information. For some reason she blames me and the whole world for Robert leaving her at the restaurant by herself. Looking out the window a black Lincoln Town car pulls up in front of the restaurant. Someone rich and famous was coming to dine and leave Leslie a big tip. The three times I saw her, her boobs greeted me first. She must have her restaurants confused. There isn't any hot wings or beer mugs sold down stairs. Mrs. Maybeline doesn't mind because lunch hour is beginning to be full of men who are a part of the Leslie fan club. Two uniform soldiers get out the black waxed car and immediately I start smiling and grabbing Kimberly so we could greet daddy. One was tall and the other was short and muscular. This is why he hasn't called or responded, he wanted to surprise us. Going down the stairs I try to catch my breath because my man is home.

Why did I cancel that hair appointment? I cannot let Leslie and her boobs be the first to greet him.

"Baby where are you?...Robert?"

I peruse the restaurant and customers are looking at me kind of strange.

"Robert I'm here baby."

It is December 12, 2013 and he know my birthday is around the corner. He's in the kitchen, I wonder what romantic scene he has created in the back for me. I knew today was going to be a unique day. It was 12/12/13 and a gentleman was playing 1213 pick four for the lottery at the gas station earlier.

"Kendra Kendra calm down Robert is not here have a seat."

"What do you mean Mrs. Maybeline? Robert is here. These are his friends right? Are you his friends?"

The two uniformed men smiles and look at Kimberly and I. "She looks just like him," the sergeant whispers to his partner. Their uniform was so crisp, decorated with pins, and wrinkle free. I could not wait to see Robert in his uniform and have him swoop me up in his arms like in the movie, An Officer and a Gentleman. I'm going to count the pins he has earned. Mrs. Maybeline began to tear up and say, "Kendra, can we go upstairs and talk?"

"Sure, why are you crying he is home now?"

As we walk upstairs Mrs. Maybeline advises Leslie to look over the floor for about thirty minutes. Sitting on the couch I begin shaking my leg because I want to hurry up and get to wherever Robert is or be surprised with my proposal.

"Kendra these gentlemen have informed me that there is some important information about Robert they would like to share." Mrs. Maybeline voice was quivering and for the first time I realized maybe Robert is not down stairs to surprise me. The short muscular officer stood in the middle of the front room and begin to speak.

My name is Officer Griffin. It is with my deepest sympathy to inform the family that Robert was in an accident during the flight drills. He was fatally injured during one of the exercises along with Sergeant Jackson at 0900 hours."

"Did you say fatally? Fatally usually means death so I would choose a different word." I explained to Officer Griffin.

"Yes Ma'am, I understand. Robert is no longer with us."

"You're lying, take me to Robert." I demand while approaching Officer Griffin. Mrs. Maybeline grabs Kimberly out of my arms for her comfort. She is looking in disbelief and is speechless. I am torn between slapping the lie out of the officer mouth or going down stairs to slap Robert for playing the worse trick in the world on me. I begin to go back down stairs and the two men stop me. "Ma'am Robert is gone. He is not down stairs."

"No! No! Don't ever say that to me."

He embraces me in a way that confirms he is telling the truth.

"Ma'am, we are sorry for your lost."

"Her lost?"

He words jolted Mrs. Maybeline out of shock.

"I spent 14 hours in labor with him. He never smoked a cigarette. He was the perfect gentlemen and I trusted you with his life. I gave you my future and you let it die. What am I going to do now? You took my heartbeat. You took my air. What am I going to do now?"

Mrs. Maybeline had a point. Robert was her son before he was my man. I needed answers.

"How could you let this happen? We were going to get married. When did it happened?"

"Ma'am Robert was expired on December 10, 2013."

"That was two days ago. You mean to tell me he has been gone for two whole days and we are just finding out about it. I thought the drills were simulated."

"They are but Robert displayed advanced comprehension so it was determined to increase his exposure to the aircraft. During the exercise Robert had a panic attack and could no longer follow the instructions from the command center and the instructor. He and Pilot Jackson expired due to the unforeseen accident.

"Nana cry. What's wrong with nana?" Kimberly wants her grandmother to stop crying. I can't take it. My head is spinning and everyone faces looks fuzzy.

When I wake up my mama has a cold white towel on my fore head and some hot green tea by the bedside. "Mama?"

"Yes baby."

"How did you get here...I had a horrible dream that Robert was dead. Mama tell me it was a dream"

"I wish I could baby, but I'm afraid I can't lie to you." Mama begins to cry and I knew it was true.

"Who has Kimberly?"

"Mrs. Maybeline has Kimberly. She says that is all she has left of Robert and asked if she could just hold her in her arms. I could not tell her no."

"Mama he was going to marry me one day. He promised Mama."

"I know Kendra and I believed him. I know you don't want to hear this but the good Lord don't make no mistakes Kendra. We must trust him that He knows best even when it makes us feel our worst."

The next couple of days Mama stayed with me and took care of Kimberly. My orange pillow was my comfort. Robert did not deserve to die like that. He was out there bettering himself for his family and his future. How do I explain to Kimberly that da da is not coming home?

I'm concerned for Mrs. Maybeline. She has had Kimberly for three days now. I am afraid to ask for her back. Robert was her only baby. She has invested so much in him and the restaurant to guarantee his success and now that dream is over. As mean as she is to me, she loves Robert and did her best to raise a responsible and respectable young man and I will always love her for that. This is just not how I thought our relationship would end. Our story was to end with gray hairs, walking canes, and us rubbing green alcohol on each other.

Trina and Krystal have called constantly but I don't have nothing in me to speak about. Trina flew back in town to lift my spirits. As she walks in my bedroom I try to smile but the pain is too heavy in my heart, just breathing is a task.

"Hey Ken, are you OK?"

"No Trina, he's gone. Robert is gone. He was the best thing that happened to me besides Jesus Christ and Kimberly."

"I know Ken and God knows. We just have to believe that God does not make any mistakes and that He will get you through this time of mourning."

"What if God made His first mistake? Trina, what's the purpose of living? I will never love another like Robert. I want to go with him Trina."

"Remember Kimberly and live for her Kendra. Live for Robert too. I'm sure he is in heaven watching over you and Kimberly. What about me how am I going to survive without you? I need you Kendra."

"Thank you for coming home to be with me?"

"My professor said I was no good sitting in glass crying during his lectures so he is allowing me to email my assignments for the next week. I love you Ken. I know it hurts."

"Do you need me to get you anything from the store? Would you like for me to cook you some of my famous tacos? Look at that a smile, tacos it is."

"Thanks Trina. I am hungry."

"Fine, I will go home and make them and be back with you a plate."

Since I was not Robert spouse I did not have any decisions during this process. Pastor Jenkins volunteered to have the funeral at the church but Mrs. Maybeline wanted it in a funeral home. Mrs. Maybeline wanted to have the funeral on a Tuesday and I wanted to have it on a Saturday.

Today Tuesday and getting prepared for Robert funeral is taking all of the strength I have to dress Kimberly and I. Protocol is to wear black, but Robert was so full of life so I decided to dress us in blue, his favorite color. It is going to be a close coffin and I think it is for the best. I want our last memory of him to be smiling and alive not lying stiff in a decorated box. As the limousine picks us up I can't help but think why is the only time I am in a limo is when someone dies? When we finally reach the funeral home Mrs. Maybeline is already inside. We are guided by the ushers to the front row to join Mrs. Maybeline and the family. The coffin is covered with an American flag and a picture of Robert on top in his uniform. Kimberly begins to say,

"Da da, Mama there's daddy." The whole churches begin to sigh at the innocent and intense plea from Kimberly to go to the picture of Robert.

"Da da sleeping Kimberly. Da da is sleeping precious. I hug Mrs. Maybeline and when I look up I see Leslie three rows back crying silently. Mama and Trina are on the same row. Mama winks at me to let me know that I can get through this and she is here to support me. All of Robert's hockey team came in their jerseys to represent his love for the sport. Robert commanders got up and told stories of how Kimberly was Robert's pride and joy and that he loved us dearly along with his parents. I heard Mrs. Maybeline say to one of her sisters that Robert dad had showed up but she could not find him anymore. It was a testament of how Robert was love and how he loved many. I don't even think he had an enemy in life. I felt honored to be chosen to love him in this dispensation of time.

A week later a letter came in the mail informing me to meet downtown at a lawyer office for the reading of a will that Robert had left. He was not even buried ten days and already things were moving really fast. Mrs. Maybeline's attitude is staring to change. She dropped Kimberly off and has not returned any of my calls. It is getting hard to distinguish if she is in mourning or just being rude as always. This letter is confusing to me so I want to discuss it with Mrs. Maybeline.

"Hello everyone, where's the boss lady?"

"She is in the back in her office" Leslie responded."

"Thanks"

As I approach her door I can see through the square glass that she is on the phone so Kimberly and I make funny faces at the door to lighten the air. After thirty seconds Mrs. Maybeline signals for us to come in.

"Hello Kendra, how are you holding up?"

"I'm taking it day by day. I should be asking you because you have had the greater loss. I want to thank you for raising such a beautiful son. He was a special man and you did a wonderful job as a parent."

"Well thank you Kendra. Now did you come down here to praise me as a parent today?"

"Actually I received a letter in the mail requesting my attendance to a reading of a will Robert left."

Mrs. Maybeline posture changed instantly and she begins to speak in a semi firm tone.

"Now Kendra we've been through this before. You and Robert were not married so there is no need for you to be present at the reading of his will. You can be briefed after the reading. No need to get you and Kimberly all worked up and out in the cold."

"Actually I think it will bring closure. The way the letter reads I don't know if I should ignore it."

Mrs. Maybeline begins to rise up from her brown leather swivel chair and sits on her desk in front of Kimberly and me. Her eyes begin to get red. Before she speaks she dusts her professional cleaned cream pants,

"Kendra I am telling you your attendance is not necessary or desired. This is family business."

My mouth opened and my eyes enlarged. In front of my baby, Robert's baby she said not to come because it was family business.

"Mrs. Maybeline, hello….. your granddaughter Kimberly is right in front of you. She can hear you." I said covering Kimberly ears.

"Look Kendra, let's be honest. When my son was here I had to put up with you but, now he is gone. Robert was always simple and gullible. But here is the reality of the situation. Big Ma looked suspicious at that baby."

"That baby?"

"Yes, that baby."

"We got Indian, Irish, and French in our family. I know my Robert was dark but all of the grand children have medium brown skin and then you come in here with this dark baby embarrassing me. It is because of you that my Robert is dead. He met you and all the plans of him opening up a second location went south. Now he is gone and all the favors and free rides are gone too. You have to carry your own weight around here or go back home to yo mama."

"Mrs. Maybeline how can you say those things in front of Kimberly? I will go home to my mama and I will see you at the reading of the will."

"Well on your way to yo mama leave the keys to my car. That's right my car ….my name on the title. The car is not yours or Robert's."

I knew she was a witch but she than morphed into an insensitive bitch. I called mama right away and told her what Mrs. Maybeline had said and did. She came over quickly and told me to grab all of our clothes and belongings. Mrs. Maybeline had purchased all of the furniture so there was not much to take. I cried the whole way back to Mama house. How could you call your grandchild an embarrassment because she is dark skin like your son? How could you kick us out for wanting to be present during the reading of Robert's last wishes? How can you be so evil that you would hate the woman that your son loved so dearly? When we pulled up to the house Kimberly was familiar with Mama's house and begins to say, "Nana house, Nana house." She instantly went in and took over the remote control and turned to cartoons. Mama had to preach to herself. She wanted to fight Mrs. Maybeline after hearing what happened. I had to stop her from grabbing the Vaseline and breading her hair to the back.

"Kendra I ain't had a fight since the seventh grade and I promise you that woman makes me want to put my hands on her." Mama was walking around the kitchen like it was a fighting ring. The only thing was missing was some boxing gloves and the referee.

"Kendra, this is what you and my grandbaby have been putting up with? Did Robert know this was going on? "

"No."

As I enter my room my favorite orange pillow welcomes me and I dive on it. It feels good to be home where I am wanted, welcomed, and loved. I begin to prepare myself mentally for another showdown with Mrs. Maybeline at the lawyer's office. After today I am confident that she has lost her marbles. I can't help it but I grab my pen and begin to write.

I'm not mad at you for leaving me but for

Loving me

I was doing just fine in life without you but

You had to smile, had to illuminate the room, had to steal my heart with your giving of yourself

You gave me hope,

Purpose,

a daughter,

and a future

But no one told me you would not be accompanying me along the journey.

Thank you for all of the memories and the honor to experience love, joy, and family.

As we sit at the table Kimberly says, "Mama da da was in my sleep." Mama and I looked at each other and was in sheer silence for thirty seconds. "What did da da say?" Mama asked.

"Da da says he love me and mommy." I smiled and I said, "That's right da da loves you and mommy. Mama shook her head and begins to eat her scramble eggs. Robert came and visited his daughter in her dreams. He was still living just not in the natural only in the spirit. It was time to go to the lawyer's office to hear the reading of the will. Downtown Chicago traffic is congested. Orange cones are everywhere merging lanes due to a highway expansion. We have to be there by 9 a.m. It's rainy and the weather is about 29 degrees. Today I will hear my Robert voice through his will. Whatever he says I will be content.

Chicago XX

The Land of Redemption

It has been years since I parked down town Chicago. It was a shocker to see that parking garages cost twenty-five dollars for six –eight hours and fifteen dollars for the first hour. As we enter the lawyer office waiting room I could not believe my eyes. Leslie and Mrs. Maybeline are sitting in the black vinyl waiting room chairs on the right side of the room. Mrs. Maybeline has a smirk on her face. She knew that was a dagger in my heart but she did not care. What happen to the "family business" BS she told me? What happened to, "this is a family matter?" When did Leslie become family? Now was not the time to address Kendra copycats but in due season. Mama said hello and Mrs. Maybeline smiled. There was a gentleman sitting two seats away from Mrs. Maybeline. He was reading the Business section of New York Times newspaper. His shoes were brown and looked Italian. Five minutes later the reception said, "Mr. Julianoski will see the Thompson family now. We all stand up and I noticed the guy folds his paper and put it in his Coach brief case and stand up as well. Curiously I asked the gentleman, "Who are you?"

"I am Robert Senior and you must be Kendra?"

"Yes sir and this is your granddaughter Kimberley Rose Thompson."

"Thank you for loving my son and making his last days joyful. He wrote me a couple of times and spoke volumes about you two. We were going to arrange a time for us all to meet. I hate we had to meet under these circumstances."

Mr. Julianoski had to give up his chair due to one extra person, Leslie. Mrs. Maybeline insisted Leslie come in for emotional and physical support. What did I ever do so bad to Mrs. Maybeline but love her son that she would cling to Leslie than me? Now she has Leslie holding her hand and handing her handkerchiefs like she is her daughter or worst Robert's girl. I want to grieve together with Mrs. Maybeline but that is impossible when I am viewed as the culprit. The lawyer clears his throat and begins to read.

I Robert Earl Thompson, of 15327 York Road, Elmhurst IL, 60126, declare that this is my last will and testament.

I revoke all prior wills and codicils.

I am unmarried but happily engaged to Kendra Latrice Springfield.

I have one child Kimberly Rose Thompson.

I give my entire interest in any personal automobiles, household goods, furnishings, tools, jewelry, clothing, and tangible articles to my mom Maybeline Thompson.

If, at my death, I have any child or children under the age of 18 and such does not have a living parent, I nominate Mrs. Denise Springfield to take guardianship.

I give said full Executor and absolute authority a discretion to direct that any, part of or all said assets bequeathed, transferred or gifted to such minor beneficiary be held in a trust until such beneficiary turns 18.

I hereby nominate my fiancé Kendra Latrice Springfield to serve as trustee.

"Now wait a minute" interjected Mrs. Maybeline. "Kendra is the trustee."

"Ma'am at the end of the reading we will answer all questions." Mrs. Maybeline sits back down and takes a Japanese fan out of her purse. She hands it to Leslie and she begins to fan her.

If this person for any reason is unable or unwilling to serve as trustee, I nominate my dad Robert Earl Thompson Sr.to serve as the trustee of such Testamentary Trust.

I hereby name Kimberly Rose Thompson the beneficiary of my life insurance policy with Liberty & Lincoln in the amount of $500,000. If she is under the age of eighteen in my expiration I appoint Kendra Latrice Johnson to be the Power of Attorney of the funds.

"Robert has also left us with a safe box with instructions to open only if something like this happened. Mr. Julianoski pulls out a royal blue velvet jewelry box. "Before I open the box I must read a letter that is accompanied with it to the family."

Dear Family and Love ones,

If this letter is being read to you then my death has transpired. I would like to thank each and every one of you for making my life on earth a blast. I will never forget the family gatherings and of course my mama's food. I hope God has a good cook in heaven because Ma to me you are the best cook in the world so He has some great shoes to fill in feeding me up here. Thank you mom for loving me and believing in me. No one will ever take your place. I knew death was a probability in joining but I wanted to overcome my fears and not be in prison by them. Dad thank you for the talks and teachings on how to be a responsible man. Even though you and mom did not work out you never missed a beat in being there for me when I needed you most and for that I thank you and love you dearly. I hope I made you proud. To Mrs. Springfield thank you for trusting me with your most precious possession, Kendra. I told you at the table that I loved her and I would be there for her and my child. I hope I have held up my end of the bargain and you can forgive me for not marrying her first. To my beautiful wife Kendra. We did not have a wedding but I knew a long time ago that whenever I left this world it would be with you in my heart. I love you so much and thank you for loving me back. Your gifts of our daughter is priceless. Inside this box is a token of my love. I asked you to marry me one day but I did not have a ring. Excuse my bad manners. Please accept this ring as a token of my love. I will not be there physically for you but hopefully the resources that have been given to you will provide an environment for productivity and peace for you and Kimberly. Lastly to Kimberly my beautiful princess. In this life you may come across some mean people but know that I love you and God loves you and always walk in love. Love conquers all. I promise to send a kiss down from heaven to you daily. Know that you were made from love. Know that you were the reason I woke up every morning. Know that if no one else accepts you for whatever reasons that God and I accepts you. I thank God for my beautiful black baby and don't let anyone make you feel bad because of your complexion or your competence.

Sincerely,

Robert Earl Thompson

Robert also wrote a poem:

I WISH I WAS A CHAIR

Oh if I knew then what I knew now

I would have chosen to be another object

An object like a chair or a table

hard, no emotions, and very sturdy

Or maybe a picture frame

Small, light, and square

But God had another plan

He chose human

And bless me with senses like

Sight, hearing, speaking, and feelings.

I learned how to survive in life.

I learned how to listen.

I learned how to speak and defend myself.

I learned how to love.

In discovering these adventures, I was introduced to happiness and sadness.

I realized for the rest of my life I would experience these feelings.

I found out every day is a gift from God and everything has an expiration date.

From your bread, to your life,

From your milk, to your wife,

So I decided to embrace each day expecting the best

I began treating each obstacle that comes with living like a test.

A Dad's Redemption

I thank God up above,

For choosing me to meet the people I have met.

Fight the people I have fought.

Love the people I have loved.

Because the best thing in life is love,

It is so wild.

It takes you up and it takes you down.

It gives you hope

It gives you strength.

The only sad part about it is, one day I know it will end.

Maybe if I was a chair someone could put me back together again.

I knew at that moment Robert was in heaven looking down on us. He showed the world and especially Mrs. Maybeline that he loved and accepted Kimberly and I. Leaving us that life insurance policy I think said it all. He wanted to show mama that he really loved me and in the end she believed him. He wanted to keep his promise to marry me one day so he purchased a ring for if he died in combat before we got married. After the reading of the will it was Q&A time and the room was silent. I wasn't clear so I asked, "Mr. Julian ski is it my understanding that Kimberly is awarded $500,000 in a trust fund until she is eighteen?"

"Not quite. Kimberley is awarded the $500k now and since she is a minor you will be the trustee."

Mrs. Maybeline stood up and came launching at Mr. Julian ski pointing her finger, "My baby would never forget about his mama. This is not Robert's will. It can't be. I will contest it. What if he has other children?"

"What are you saying Mrs. Maybeline? My Robert would never lie to me. I would have known."

Mrs. Maybeline stormed out of the lawyer's office with her hands blocking further communication. Leslie followed closely.

"I did not even know he had a will." I pleaded to Robert Sr.

"Kendra, you did nothing wrong. These are Robert's wishes. He loved you and was constantly thinking about you and his daughter. I know my son loved me and I am not mad that he left money to you. You have to raise his little princess and I am proud I raise a young man that was so responsible even unto the end. The truth is Maybeline and I are well off. We don't need the money."

"Thanks sir."

"Call me dad. And you little princess call me granddad." Robert Sr. grabs Kimberly checks and she begins to laugh. As I look for mama she is in the corner smiling and talking to God underneath her breath.

"Mama are you OK?"

"Yes, Robert has truly displayed today his love for you. In the beginning I could not tell if he was going to be a disappointment in your life but the good Lord sent you an angel. May God bless & rest his soul."

As I leave the building the suns comes out of a big gray cloud and shines right on Kimberly and I. The winds blows the scent of Chanel my way and I stop in my tracks and look up in the sky and smile. I know he is here with me at this moment and I know he will always be there for us. Even though he was unable to make me an honest woman. He has partnered with God and secured my daughter future and I will forever be thankful and I will protect that inheritance from Mrs. Maybeline and Leslie. I need a lawyer......

About The Author

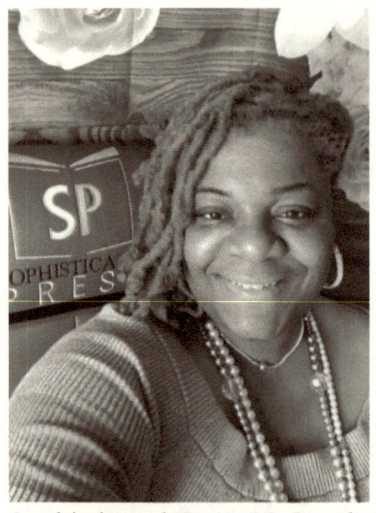

Renetta Gunn Stevens is the CEO of Sophisticated Press LLC. She has helped numerous writers complete their dreams of becoming a Published Writer.

Renetta Gunn-Stevens knew at an early age she was an entrepreneur, writer, and critical thinker. After several endeavors, she aligned her purpose and passion. She built Sophisticated Press LLC to help others share their stories and leave a legacy through books and businesses. With five books stirring inside her imagination, she decided to start a publishing company and become her first customer with the following titles, A Dad's Redemption, Kingdom Speaking In The Boardroom, and 10 ways To Eliminate Debt. She is a ghostwriter, pioneer, and trendsetter that is making publishing accessible and affordable.

Renetta has been featured on Freedem Radio as a special guest and continue to present workshops globally to educate writers on the publishing process. She is a Competent Communicator granted by Toastmasters International, where she held multiple positions including President. Her hobbies include spending time with her wonderful family, mentoring, writing, and publishing books.

Upcoming Titles

Kingdom Speaking In The Boardroom

Jesus Sale: How To Sell Without Selling Out Jesus

Crown Jacker

Booking for trainings or conferences:

Attn: Renetta Gunn-Stevens

Po Box 831

Elmhurst IL, 60126

Email: sophisticatedpress@gmail.com

www.ingramcontent.com/pod-product-compliance
Lightning Source LLC
Chambersburg PA
CBHW030322020726
47493CB00004B/1129